SLOW BURN

Sam B. Morgan

LooseId.

ISBN 13: 978-1-62300-781-2
SLOW BURN
Copyright © November 2014 by Sam B. Morgan
Originally released in e-book format in January 2014

Cover Art by Mina Carter
Cover Layout and Design by Fiona Jayde

Printed in the U.S.A. by
Lightning Source, Inc.
1246 Heil Quaker Blvd
La Vergne TN 37086
www.lightningsource.com

DEDICATION

This story is dedicated to both of you, for the therapy of your journey and growth, and proving once more that every child deserves love so they become adults capable of loving.

ACKNOWLEDGMENT

A million billion thanks to the Captain, for knowing what's what; Detective Ms. Badass, for keeping it on the level; Jeanette Grey, for the support and techno savvy skills; and Rory Olsen, on-point editor who takes the raw material and makes it shine.

CHAPTER ONE

Brody thumped his fist against the paint-chipped front door, loving the way the hinges groaned in protest. Next to him, Lamont let out a long-suffering sigh and shifted on his feet.

"What?" Brody banged again.

Lamont didn't grace him with another look of doom. Instead he straightened his tie and fanned the sides of his suit jacket against the oppressive Charleston heat. "You want to dial it back a notch?" he asked. "We're here for questioning, not a raid."

"No. We're here wasting our damn time on a dead-end lead."

"No lead is a waste," Lamont argued, leaning out over the stoop to peer inside a window.

"Maybe not, but this kid, Kenny? He's not our Strangler."

"He's got priors."

"So do half the kids in this neighborhood. He doesn't make sense as a suspect. Not to mention when I found the first DB, he would've been, what? Fourteen?" Brody shook his head at his partner. "No way in hell is he the Strangler."

"I'm not saying I disagree." Lamont swiped at the sweat on his forehead. "I'm saying we got a lead. Helluva lot more than what we've had the last year, so it's our job to check."

They were only knocking on Kenny's door under captain's orders, and his reasons reeked of coddling the press. Brody would love to tell him where he could shove his reasons. This was his case. From the night he'd found the first victim when he was a shiny new uni, right up until now. Sure, leads were scarce, but this was bullshit.

"This is bullshit," he grumbled aloud, turning to eye the street behind them.

"So you've said. All through lunch, in the car on the drive over here—"

"And not once did you disagree with me. So Kenny is from..." He made a point of looking around at the run-down neighborhood. "Here. You know that doesn't mean jack."

This time Lamont did look over. His dark eyes softened as he gave a small nod. He was from the same neighborhood, and he saw the holes in this lead just as clearly, but he was playing good cop. Brody walked the fine path of keeping the brass happy, but he couldn't manage it with a smile quite like his partner's. He'd follow this bullshit lead so the captain didn't bust a vessel, but tonight he'd be knee-deep in the files, looking for something that might actually catch a killer.

This time Lamont stepped forward and knocked while Brody stared a hole through the door.

"You hoping for X-ray vision, man?" Lamont tried the handle. "Quit scowling. You're scaring the door. What do you think? Not home?"

"Car's in the driveway." His mood shifted as he focused on the familiar prickle of instinct. Time to break out the old patrol-cop skills: Yell *Cops!* See who scatters.

"Police! Open up!" Brody banged on the door with both fists.

There was a beat of silence, then a soft *thump* followed by a screen door slam from the back.

"Shit. He's running!" Lamont ran for the car while Brody leaped off the front stoop and sprinted for the side gate.

Damn it! It'd been too long since he jumped feetfirst into a full-on foot chase. Brody's legs protested as he pushed them into high gear. Homicide tended to deal with bodies that didn't move fast. Or at all.

He caught sight of the runner, recognizing him as Kenny. Barely nineteen, carrying a lot less muscle, and hauling ass toward the back. Brody closed in only for Kenny to jump the fence in a blur of red T-shirt and denim.

"Shit." Brody pumped it harder, grabbing the crumbling planks and launching himself over. He landed hard on his feet and reached for his radio, continuing down the gravel road that ran between neighborhoods.

"In pursuit...heading west on Simons."

He heard Lamont's voice in response as he gained some ground. The kid had a lead now and knew the area. Home-field advantage. He hoped he didn't start darting through yards.

Kenny ducked into the side gate of another house.

"Fuck." Brody followed him through the gate.

The backyard was a hazard area of tall grass and scrap metal. He dodged half of a rusty car and followed the kid through the opposite gate. A fully operational car narrowly missed Kenny as he sprinted out into the road. Blast of a loud horn, but he kept moving.

"Now cutting through the grocery-store parking lot, headed west." Brody followed; the only thing in view was Kenny's black cap as he ran past parked cars.

Brody was starting to feel it, thighs burning, his body praying for Kenny to make a mistake. He pushed it, and geography finally caught up with the kid.

Kenny ran himself into a corner. Wire fencing blocked off the path straight ahead, concrete walls on both sides. Panting hard, Brody raised his hands when it looked like Kenny was going to make a leap for it.

"Stop! We just want to talk."

Kenny shifted on his feet, eyes darting from side to side, taking in his surroundings.

Brody took a couple of deep breaths, wanting his voice to be calm and even. "Kenny."

He flinched and made a jump for the wall.

Brody leaped and caught his shirt. Kenny fought for balance and lost. He fell back, grabbing Brody on the way. They came down hard and awkward. Kenny landed on top, and pain shot through Brody's left knee.

Pop!

"Fuck!" Brody rolled but clung to his catch. He clenched down on the pain. Thank God for adrenaline. "Don't fucking move," he growled at the boy, hauling himself up.

He pushed his weight into Kenny's back, managing to reach around and pull out his cuffs. Blinking through the throbbing haze of whatever the hell had just happened to his knee, he slapped the cuffs on and reached for his radio.

"This is Brody. One in custody at the Piggly Wiggly on Meeting Street. Requesting assistance."

He dug his elbow into Kenny's back. "Don't fucking move," he told the kid again. He wasn't in the habit of being an ass with suspects, but Kenny hadn't come quiet and now something major was going down with his knee.

Lamont pulled up in the Crown Vic and jumped out. Brody let out a groan of pain and relief when Lamont pulled the kid up.

"You all right?" Lamont searched the boy but still managed to triage Brody with a glance.

"Yeah. Just get him in."

His partner's eyes narrowed, but he loaded Kenny into the back of the car.

Brody rolled back onto the pavement and tried to will the pain away. He closed his eyes and immediately felt the shadow of Lamont's tall frame blocking the sun.

"Fine my ass. Come on, I'll help you up."

Brody squinted up at Lamont's huge, out-held hand. He took it, but when he stood and tried to put weight on the knee, it buckled.

Brody hissed and had to cling to his partner to keep from dropping like a rock.

"Mmm-hmm. Fine my *ass*," Lamont repeated. "I remember the look of that shit from football. You've blown out your knee, my friend." He reached for his radio and requested a paramedic.

"I'm told you I'm fine. I'll be *fine*," Brody grumbled.

But the older detective ignored him, tugging him to lean more on his arm as he walked them over to the passenger seat.

"The bus won't be long." Lamont sat him down and stood beside the car. "Just sit there and shut up."

Being off the ground didn't help the pain at all. Lying, sitting, standing—it all hurt like hell. Brody groaned and laid his head against the back of the seat. Chasing that kid had screwed him. He'd torn something up like a damn champ. Fucking perfect.

"Sonuvabitch," he hissed as he tried to shift in the seat. "I need a new partner."

A flash of white teeth from Lamont. "I just *saved* your ass, and you're complaining?"

They both turned their heads toward the paramedics pulling into the parking lot.

"Yeah." Brody grimaced as another bolt of pain ran through his leg. "But I need a young one to do all the damn running. Because I think my knee is fucked."

CHAPTER TWO

A month later...

"**S**orry I'm late." Zack rushed through the door, clipboard in hand.

He never ran late. People were accustomed to waiting when it came to health care, and he loved the surprise on their faces when he arrived on time for their physical therapy. Being ten minutes late for his last appointment of the day crawled all over him. The surly, broad-shouldered, boxing-champ look-alike currently death glaring him didn't help.

"I was hoping you'd forget," the man muttered, hand over his bound left knee, his dark eyebrows wrinkled at the sight of Zack.

Right. *This* guy.

His coworker, Matt, had told him all about this patient yesterday. Douglas Brody, detective for the City of Charleston, blew out his ACL on the job. Went by Brody, uncooperative, making no progress, all around pain-in-the-ass patient. Matt's words. He'd tried working with Brody but insisted on passing him off after just a few weeks.

"You planning to start with the same monkey tricks as your friend or just stare me into being able to run again?" Brody asked.

Zack hadn't realized he was staring. In certain other circumstances, Zack would absolutely stare at a man like Detective Brody. But not here and not with an ill-tempered patient. Not with any patient.

"Well?" Brody asked, his body bowing up like a snake ready to strike.

Matt wasn't kidding about the attitude.

"They're not monkey tricks, Detective. They're exercises meant to increase your range of motion and strength." Zack noted the flash of recognition in Brody's eyes when he'd called him detective. Figured he'd like that. Brody loved his job and wanted to get back to it ASAP. He'd made that much clear enough that even a slack PT like Matt made a note in his file. Motivating factor. Every patient needed it.

"By the way, I'm Zack, your new physical therapist. Nice to meet you too, and yes, I will get you up and running again. We'll start on the platform." Zack walked to the raised area in the center of the room and waited.

Brody didn't budge. Just sat there giving him the stink eye.

For someone so dedicated to being a detective and claiming readiness to get back to work, it made no sense that he wasn't fully committed to therapy. Maybe there was some other issue here, the squishy stuff that went beyond physical recovery. Matt didn't "deal with that shit," as he put it, but Zack didn't mind a challenge. Zack found that difficult patients generally had a reason. Brody was probably in a lot of pain, and the meds definitely made you a different person. He looked like a normally capable guy and, with his job and...physique, clearly physical. Suddenly taking away his ability to walk would make someone like him an asshole. Zack worked in health care; he expected to deal with people who weren't at their best.

"We're over here," Zack said again, waving his new patient over with an intentionally over-the-top smile.

Brody made his way to the platform with the heavy *clunk-clink* of crutches. He wasn't even using those correctly.

"Hold all your weight up with your hands, not under your arms."

"What?" Brody scowled, coming to a stop.

Zack stepped forward and pushed Brody's shoulders back, feeling his whole body stiffen at the physical contact. He stood up straight and then leaned away.

"No, not leaning back. Up straight. Like this," Zack said,

nudging him forward. "Press down on your hands, using the strength of the entire arm to help hold your weight as you walk. Keeps your posture straight and you won't pinch a nerve under your arm."

Brody kept on scowling and clunked even louder the last few paces, but he used the crutches correctly.

"You're welcome. Now, we're going to start with range of motion. Face the platform, and we'll work on bending the knee. You can use the crutches for balance if you need them."

Brody tossed the crutches down with a metallic *clang*. He grunted as he reached for the bar, slowly getting himself into position.

"Okay"—Zack moved to stand closer, eyes on the offending leg—"bend your right knee for me, please, bringing the foot toward the back of your thigh."

Brody bent his knee, barely able to keep his balance and not even getting his shin parallel to the floor. Zack watched as Brody's entire body trembled with the effort, face red from both pain and exertion. After already having had weeks of therapy, this was unacceptable.

"What have you been working on at home, Mr. Brody? Because you should be further along than this."

Zack expected another scowl, but Brody didn't look at him. He stared straight ahead and spoke low and cool.

"It's *Detective* Brody or just Brody."

Dammit! Zack knew that. Matt had mentioned he didn't like Mr. and sure as hell didn't like Douglas. He added a note to the file.

"Okay, Brody. It's obvious you haven't been doing your exercises at home. You should at least be able to bend your knee to here." Zack reached down, and, with one hand supporting the knee, he pushed Brody's shin up, parallel to the floor.

Brody wobbled and grabbed for support. His hand landed on Zack's shoulder, and he fumbled with it before snatching his hand away to hold on to the platform.

It was an odd reaction, since Zack was there for exactly that reason. He'd been used as a crutch, a wall, a seat, a catcher—okay that last one could sound a little pervy—a weight, a prop, whatever was needed during a session. It was part of being a physical therapist. It was a hands-on job. About as hands-on as it got.

Maybe that was this guy's problem. Either he had personal space issues or the idea of another man touching him freaked him out, to the point he couldn't even do therapy. Well too bad; they had to come into *some* contact, and all the female PTs were booked up.

"I'm doing the exercises," Brody bit out as he turned and hopped to sit down. "Fat lot of good it's done me. Still can't do a damn thing, because they're bullshit exercises like knee bends and stationary bike rides." He practically snarled at the mention of them. "I have a job to do and no time to waste on a bike going no-fucking-where, so you better be smarter than Matt Whatshisface and come up with a plan, or I'm telling the department to find a new place to spend their money."

Yeah. This guy's issues were so much more than any phobia.

"Then you're in luck, Brody." Zack used his name intentionally. "I am *a lot* smarter than Matt and a lot more persistent. Now get off your butt and bend that knee again. This time, admit defeat and use the crutches. Next visit you better be able to balance without it, or you're going to have to hold on to me. Like it or not."

Brody's chin shot up, his glare matching Zack's. Zack wasn't going to back down. He'd dealt with plenty of hardheaded patients. Even if there was no doubt Brody was going to be the hardest, both in physique and disposition, Zack wasn't budging.

"Shit," Brody said as he pushed off the platform. Their eyes remained locked even as he grabbed the crutches and stood, just a couple of inches short of being nose to nose with Zack.

Zack looked down at him. Brody was probably used to being the big guy in the room, coming in at about six foot two from the look of it, but Zack was six four.

Take that and smoke on it, Mr. Too Much Testosterone.

Okay, that was probably more than a little childish.

"Surprised you didn't flinch at my *profanity*." Brody put on a Matt-like snotty voice, so scary in its accuracy Zack had to bite back a grin. "Your little friend had a coronary if I even said hell."

"He's not my friend; we work at the same clinic. There's a big difference. And I prefer you keep the cursing to a minimum as we do have other patients. That being said, some of this will hurt like *hell*, so I personally don't mind."

The corner of Brody's mouth twitched, almost like he would smile, but Zack figured the man wasn't capable.

They ran through more range of motion, Zack showing him how he *must* do this at home, regardless of how he felt about it.

And to take regular ibuprofen, keep the swelling down.

When Brody mentioned he wasn't taking *anything* for pain, saying it made him "feel funny," Zack nearly fell over backward. He was only *just* out of surgery, and without analgesia, the pain must be immense. No wonder he was being a bit of an ass.

Well, "bit of" was being nice.

Zack chided him, giving him the basic lecture about inflammation while dropping two pills in Brody's hand and waiting to make sure he swallowed both.

They moved on; Zack skipped the easy stuff and went right into resistance and finally strengthening.

"We'll work around the stationary bike since you made it clear you hate it," he told Brody, "but this exercise is nonnegotiable." He wrapped the Velcro leg weight around Brody's ankle, the detective frowning down at him the entire time.

"No cheating by leaning on the crutches," Zack said. "Just use them for balance and lift the leg like we did earlier."

Brody did the first few easy enough, but somewhere around lifts five and six, his leg started to shake. The quadriceps of his left leg had already weakened. It didn't take long for that to happen. What you didn't use, you'd lose.

"Come on," Zack encouraged. "You can knock out ten. Keep going."

A crease marred Brody's forehead, but he didn't stop. He struggled through the last two, the effort making his whole frame shake, but he finished.

"Excellent," Zack said, more pleased with a few simple leg

lifts than he should be.

Brody didn't look happy at all. "Pretty fucking sad if you ask me," he said. "All I can do to manage a few lousy lifts, when I used to..." He shook his head. "It's pathetic."

The man had done about five other exercises prior. It was normal to wear out. Did he expect perfection every time? A patient like Brody, you didn't ask that. He'd only get mad again and shut down. Instead you challenged.

"Well, if it's all you can do, it's all you can do." Zack shrugged.

"It's not all I can do." Brody snapped his head up to glare. "Look at me. I'm in better shape than anyone in our department. Does it look like this should be a fucking challenge?"

No, it certainly did not, but Zack was trying *very* hard not to notice. "No, but you're recovering from a game-changing injury. You've got to put in the work to get your strength back. Getting hung up on being injured and throwing a pity party doesn't help. And honestly, it doesn't suit you."

"Screw you."

"No, thanks." He let the success roll off him. He was getting Brody to want it. "You ready to try the machine? Might be easier on you."

"No." Brody looked forward, his jaw working like he wanted to bite Zack's head off. "I want to do ten more of these."

Zack waved his hand like he was welcome to try and fought off a smile of victory. He knew Brody was the type to rise to the prove-it method.

Brody took a deep breath, his wide chest rising and falling before he lifted his foot again, up and down, his legs still shaking, the effort making his face flush. By the time he reached the tenth rep, his whole body was trembling.

Zack's inexcusably but perpetually pervy subconscious pointed out what else made a man's body tremble like that. He promptly told it to shut the hell up.

"Good stuff!" he exclaimed, focusing on Brody's success. "Ten more reps. Nothing pathetic in that."

A wanna-be smile crossed Brody's face before retreating into permanent hiding. "Better than nothing, I guess."

"Way to celebrate success." Zack bit his lips as the smart-ass reply spilled out. But damn, were all cops this intense? "Let's rest it for a bit," he said, knowing if he posed it as a question, Brody would refuse. Better not to give him any options.

Brody crutched over to the platform and sat. Zack couldn't resist.

"So am I smarter than Matt, or are you still shopping around for a new clinic tomorrow?" he asked.

Brody grumbled something unintelligible, shifting his weight on the platform. "Jury's still out. I'll let you know," he deadpanned.

Zack laughed despite himself. The fact that the man was *this* serious was funny.

"Now my injury is amusing?" Brody scowled, his voice cold again.

"No." Zack shook his head and sat with a decent space between them. He grinned and refused to be antagonized into reacting. "Elevate it," he said instead, motioning to Brody's leg.

"What?"

"After working your knee, you need to elevate your leg. Up here." He patted the platform between them. When Brody didn't move, Zack reached down and lifted it for him. Brody tensed again, and Zack bit back a remark.

The man had some serious physical boundary and mood issues. There was no doubt he'd baited Matt at every turn. But Zack was a better PT than Matt, and he wasn't going to be played. He wasn't going to lose this battle either. No way in hell. If it made him want to yank his hair out, he was going to get Detective Brody back up to department standards and then some. Or go bald trying.

"Better?" he asked, noticing the crease on Brody's forehead as it smoothed out.

"'S all right."

"Jeez." Zack laughed again, unable to keep it all in.

Brody glowered some more, this time like he was waiting on an explanation.

"Are you always this ornery, or is it the injury, or because Matt annoyed you? You'd swear I was asking you to gnaw off your own leg."

Brody jerked his gaze to Zack, a quirk toying with the edge of his mouth. Finally he shook his head. "It's the knee. I don't do sick well. Sick or injured or otherwise slowed down in any way. This"—he indicated his knee like it disgusted him—"needs to be fixed. Quick. I have a job to do, and your buddy Matt's bullshit stretching wasn't getting me anywhere."

"I told you, he's not my bu—"

"Yeah, yeah," Brody cut him off. "Your coworker. Whatever. But this kind of workout is...it's better."

"So glad you approve. Because it's time for round two."

Zack let Brody lower his own leg off the platform and get himself up with the crutches. They went right back to work and finished up on the machines. By the time they were done, Brody had worked up a good sweat and looked ready to keel over. He'd feel it tomorrow, but it was time well spent.

"Twenty minutes elevated with this ice pack," Zack told him, setting him up on one of the tables in a recovery room, "then you're free to go."

Instead, after he finished his session of RICE, Brody showed up near the back of the clinic, where Zack was putting away weights.

"Hey, you lost?" he asked. "Surprised you didn't bolt as soon as your twenty minutes were up." How long had Brody wandered around before finding him back here?

"I don't bolt much lately." Brody stood there, shifting his weight on his crutches like he had a lot more to say. "So do I just show up day after tomorrow, or do you actually have some kind of appointment system here?"

"Oh!" Zack shook his head and walked out of the equipment room to stand with Brody in the hall. "They'll get you scheduled out front. Just tell them you need to come in Thursday afternoon."

"I'm not getting stuck with Matt again," Brody protested. "I can stretch my hamstring by my damn self. I want you. You said you'd get me up and running again. I hope you meant it, because I don't screw around. I've got six more weeks till duty. That gives you a month and a half to fix this and prove yourself right."

"No, that gives *us* a month and a half."

"Whatever. We've got to get me back up to code. Seems like you know what you're doing, so don't make me wrong. I don't like to be wrong."

Zack wasn't sure if he should be flattered or scared. A little of both, to be honest. "Six weeks ought to be enough to get you to light duty, but you'll have to keep it up after that, if you want to move furth—"

"Good. I'll be here Thursday. Four o'clock. Don't be late this time." With that, Brody turned and crutched his way down the hall.

"Nice doing business with you too, Detective," Zack muttered as he watched him go.

He was already among Zack's most memorable patients after only one session. He was going to be the patient Zack told war stories about; he just knew it.

Brody turned toward the exit doors and had to stop to hit the auto-open button. As he waited, he tried scratching at his knee around the immobilizer. Skin always itched like crazy as it healed. He leaned over to get at it, his damp T-shirt clinging to his sculpted shoulders, his muscled lats, and the perfect curvature of his biceps.

Something Zack had spent the last hour ignoring was now completely undeniable. Detective Brody was built like a brick house. Body to die for. But he was a patient, probably straight and homophobic as fuck. Zack was not going down that road again. It was full of potholes and deadly drop-offs—all of which he'd hit and fallen over before, with the scars to prove it.

No friggin' thanks.

There was no way to lie and claim the man wasn't scorching hot, though. He had the ass of an underwear model, for crying out loud. Probably the six-pack to match. Mercy damn.

But silent admiration was one thing; entertaining the idea was another. It was not worth the pain and angst.

Not even for an ass like that.

CHAPTER THREE

B rody poked his fork into the remains of his chicken parmesan. The more he messed with it, the more it started to look like a crime scene.

And there went his appetite.

"You're not going to finish the chicken parm?" Lamont asked, his plate already clean. "You love the chicken parm here."

"Not that hungry," Brody confessed. But what if that contributed to muscle loss? He forced down another bite.

"Probably the pain meds. That'll pass once you're off them."

"I'm not on any pain meds," Brody said.

Lamont's eyebrows eased up. "None? At all?"

"Well, Advil at my PT's insistence. But none of the hard stuff, not since a few days after surgery. Made me feel like shit. I'm not putting that crap in my system. Fuck it, I'd rather deal with the pain." Even if it kept him up nights and made the day after PT miserable. The pain would pass. It had to.

Lamont chuckled, a great big baritone sound. "Suit yourself. You going for Hard Motherfucker of the Year or something? Because I can tell you right now, I already won that title just for being your partner."

Brody smiled.

"There it is!" Lamont pointed, laughing even more. "Haven't seen it in weeks, but I knew your face wasn't broken."

Brody gave him the bird.

"I miss you too, man," said Lamont.

"Yeah." Brody snorted. "Sure."

"How much longer before you get back?"

"Another week before desk duty, but it'll be almost two months before they consider putting me back on active. Screwed myself over perfectly, huh? It's bullshit, but when I pushed, Captain started sputtering like bad plumbing. I think he likes me being on leave."

It was Lamont's turn to fidget with his empty plate. He knew how tough this was on Brody. He tried to make light of it, tried to keep Brody from getting down, but no one knew him like his partner.

"Maybe you'll heal up quicker than they think. You're already in better shape than most. You never know. Said you've got a good therapist now too, so—"

"*Physical* therapist. Don't call him a therapist. Makes it sound like I'm getting my head examined. And he's all right. Better than the last one." Truth was he seemed pretty damn dedicated to his job, but Brody withheld his approval. Further investigation was required before he went so far as to say he was "good" at his job.

"So what's new in the zoo?" Brody got down to the other reason he called Lamont for lunch. It was good seeing his partner, but he'd lost touch with the streets and that had to be corrected today. The captain only gave him a high-level PC version of what he was missing. Brody wanted the full unedited.

"You know"—Lamont looked around and shrugged, the telltale sign that he was about to lie—"same old, same old. Nothing going on but the rent."

"Bullshit," Brody said again. "What happened? And don't you lie to me, or I'll call Felicia."

"Damn," Lamont mumbled and leaned in. "That's low, siccing my wife on me."

He stalled, so Brody leveled a warning glare at him.

"I didn't want to say anything with you still...y'know..."

"*Lamont*," he snapped.

Lamont blurted out four simple words. "The Strangler struck again."

Brody felt his stomach plummet and land in his already sore knee. "Shit. When?" The question pulled the air from his lungs.

"Last night. I figured you'd seen it in the papers or on the news, and that's why you wanted to have lunch."

"No. I...I didn't see either today. Yet. Save me the trouble."

"The vic's another coed, but from Southern College this time. Visiting a friend downtown. On the way back to her friend's apartment after a party."

"Shit," Brody repeated and pushed his plate away, any chance of finishing lunch now long gone. "Different school but still downtown. Same MO?"

"Yep. Wallet gone and strangled by something other than hands. Leather rope. Belt? It'll be a while before we get lab results."

"Any other assault?"

"Well..."

Brody perked up.

"She tested positive for fluids, but there was no sign of struggle. We're thinking on her way back from a party? Maybe she was with someone prior to the attack. Asked around and there was a guy, but no one likes him as a suspect. They got him to test anyway, so they can rule him out."

Brody ground his teeth together before asking, "You mean brass isn't automatically jumping on the guy she was with before she got murdered? No full focus on the fucking boyfriend? What a novel fucking idea. And where was Kenny? He have the slightest link to the girl?"

"Easy." Lamont held up his hands. "I'm just the messenger here."

"Sorry." He rubbed at his forehead. Of course this would happen when he was off duty, leaving him unable to do a damn thing but imagine all the ways he'd work this new case and the fact he couldn't do any of it.

"To answer your question, no. And I think they're warming up to your theory now since the three vics are totally unrelated."

"Four," Brody corrected him. "That's four victims now."

Lamont opened his mouth to argue, but one look from Brody and he clamped it shut.

"I hear ya, man. Four."

Four victims. The names of whom ran through Brody's head for the rest of the day, the way the images of their faces floated through his mind every night. Jennifer Martin, the first one over ten years ago, Michelle Cortez five years later, Tiffany Rush a few months ago, and now another one.

"What's her name?" Brody asked.

"Don't do this. You need to focus on your knee. On getting better."

"Fuck my knee. Her name, Lamont."

Lamont glanced over at the people sitting nearest to them and kept his eyes on them as he answered. "Amber. Amber Sloan."

Brody repeated the name three times in his head so he'd never forget it. The Strangler was escalating, but the victims remained the same. All college girls. All with bright futures. All of it wasted by someone he had yet to stop. The fact that he wasn't there right now, on the job, finding the bastard responsible, ate him alive.

---*---

Brody caught his reflection in the window of the PT clinic as he hobbled up.

Hobbled was right. It made him want to throw the crutches through the damn door. He did not have time to be down. He had a case to work. *His* case. The Strangler had always been his case in one way or another.

He was the patrol officer who had found the first victim. Jennifer Martin. Dumped like garbage on the side of a through street. She was his first DB after only a few months on the force. She was far from his last, but fuck if she wasn't the one he'd never forget.

If he was at least on light duty, he could look at the latest case. Do some interviews. Something. Crutching around like this, on paid leave, he was impotent. An invalid incapable of doing what he did best. The *only* thing he did. Without the job, he had nothing.

"This is bullshit," he growled as he reached the automatic double doors. An entire waiting room of people turned to stare like he'd kicked in the doors. To hell with them.

This time when he signed in, the lady sent him straight back to the open PT area. Zack sat there waiting, big smile on his tan face as soon as he saw Brody.

Brody wanted to say to hell with him as well. The guy was too nice. No, not nice. Nice wasn't the right word.

Decent.

"Detective Brody," Zack said, standing up. There was a lot of him when he stood. Brody didn't have to look up to many people, and he wasn't sure how he felt about it now, especially given the situation.

"Just calling me Brody will do."

"Works for me."

Of course it did. *Everything* probably worked for Zack.

"We'll get started with the flexibility again. Come on over here."

Brody could be an ass like before, but it hadn't worked then and it probably wouldn't now. He'd tossed out rounds of bad-attitude bullets last time, and Zack said nothing. He'd wanted to; Brody could see it in his eyes. He'd probably had the word *asshole* on silent repeat in his brain the whole session, but he never acted on it. He wasn't going to take the bait and give Brody the chance to let loose.

Too bad, because today he could use the release. He wanted someone to take the brunt of his wrath for one more girl losing her life, but it shouldn't be Zack. Besides, if he worked with the guy instead of against, maybe he'd get back on active that much faster.

"We've got a lot of work to do," Brody said. The drive to get back to work felt like ants under his skin.

"You're telling *me*. So are you going to get over here today or...?" Zack prompted, tapping a pen against his clipboard.

"Hang on. I don't move as fast as I used to." Brody crutched over.

Playing cooperative was tricky. Especially with someone like Zack. He wanted to max out his PT and be 110 percent ASAFP. But cooperating meant there was the danger of liking the guy. He had that air about him. That I'm-everybody's-buddy quality. Brody didn't need a buddy. Especially not one like Zack.

He reached the platform, and Zack nodded to the crutches.

"Told you today would be sans crutches. Drop 'em and give me ten."

Brody cut his gaze over and tossed down the crutches. He could do this, and he was not going to give Zack the satisfaction of seeing him wobble.

He banged out ten, albeit slow, knee raises. Then, for spite, he did a couple more.

"Nice." Zack grinned in a show of perfect, bright white teeth. "Somebody's been practicing and working hard at home. I approve."

True. He had. But Brody wasn't going to be proud that he noticed.

"Okay, hotshot." Zack walked over to one of the benches. "It's time to turn the challenge up a notch. Bring it on over here."

Brody eyed the bench and the ankle weights of different sizes. He could only imagine the kind of fresh hell this was going to be, but if it got him on the job faster—bring it on.

"Come on." Zack grinned.

He made it a few steps.

"Not without the crutches!" Zack warned.

It was too late. Brody's knee had already betrayed him.

The pain shot through his left leg, and he lurched right to overcompensate. He was headed south when Zack grabbed him, just in time. He took Brody by the arm, keeping him from stumbling, and tucked himself under to give Brody some leverage.

"Damn, dude, sorry. I meant only stretches without the crutches, not walking. You don't go anywhere without the crutches. Not until I say it's okay."

Brody shifted his weight, uncomfortable with being this close, but there was nowhere for him to go. He could make a fool of himself and end up doing a face or ass plant or he could just hang on to Zack, hard muscles and all, and let him help. He opted for the latter.

"Come on. Hang on to me, and I'll grab your crutches."

Brody did exactly that, hanging on to Zack's arm and shoulder. The guy was built solid, exactly how he looked. Hard, like Brody, but leaner. Leaner and taller.

It was something Brody had noted the moment he'd met the guy. Something he didn't want to think about.

"Here we go. Don't hop. Put your weight on me like I'm the crutch."

He felt like the biggest kind of fool standing on one foot, clinging to a man like Zack. He tried not to cringe at the feel of Zack's arm beneath his T-shirt, the solid curve of his shoulder. The cringe wasn't about disgust—at least not at Zack. The cringe came from fear and loathing. Fear that Zack...anyone... might see what Brody thought about this. What he *really* thought about Zack's sculpted arms or the rest of his tall, athletic build. The loathing was because he needed to focus on more important things. Work. Not some hot guy with great legs.

That was why Brody didn't think about it. Because if he didn't think about it, he wouldn't wonder what Zack felt like underneath his clothes. He wouldn't imagine his hands, how rough or smooth his touch might be. He wouldn't question that mouth. Would it be demanding and harsh or giving and soft? He wouldn't have to be frustrated at himself for wondering or ashamed of his cowardice for doing nothing about it.

Zack bent over, picking up the crutches and, in the process, brushing his ass against Brody's leg. It only sent his fear into overdrive. That, coupled with feeling completely useless and about as powerful as a bug stuck to the car windshield, made Brody's ability to play nice snap.

He grabbed at the crutches as soon as they were within reach and moved away from Zack as fast as he could. On crutches it was anything but nonchalant as he wobbled and attempted to find footing.

Zack's decent-guy, health-care professional instincts leaped into gear, and he steadied Brody with a hand on his shoulder. A large hand with long, capable fingers, warm and tan as the rest of him.

Brody snarled. "I'm not an invalid. I *can* stand. I've got standing down to a goddamn art."

The sting of shock across Zack's face was satisfying. Temporarily. Then Brody felt like an even bigger asshole.

Zack probably wondered who he'd screwed over to deserve this lunatic patient. But Zack, ever the professional, hid the look and replaced it with a wave of calm.

"Never said you were, Brody. Now, with the crutches, have a seat, and we'll do ten leg lifts with weights."

There was no hint of pissed off or like he'd given up. Just straight up and down to business.

Brody figured he owed him an apology, so he gave him twenty.

——*——

Yep. Brody won most difficult patient he'd ever had. Hands down. Not because of his knee injury but because of the ginormous chip on his shoulder. Second place was still Mrs. Jefferson after her hip replacement. Woman hated everyone and everything, up to and including Zack's hair. Which was just plain crazy; Zack's hair was awesome.

"Good work. Keep it going," he said as Brody hit ten, but the SOB kept going.

Brody took the cake. Zack didn't know what to expect next. Pissed off one second, working his ass off the next. Improving, then acting like it irritated the hell out of him that he did so. It was dizzying trying to keep up with someone who was all about trying, then shifted to complete asshole with a penchant for trying to provoke, then to—

Brody wiped the sweat at his forehead and swept it into his closely cut hair, making the dark brown almost black.

Zack lost the point he was trying to make with himself. Brody's hair was fairly awesome also. He shook off the thought.

Brody reached for the towel over the end of the bar and finished wiping his face before frowning up at the clock. The man frowned *a lot*.

"We need to hurry this up if I'm going to finish this set today."

Zack walked up and leaned over the end of the bar, not too close but enough to make note of the way Brody's left thigh trembled from the effort. Zack reached for the water bottle he'd been carrying around for him. Handing it over, he nodded to the clock. "How about a short break first?"

Brody took the bottle and drank deeply, water running over the day's worth of stubble and down the angled jaw. Zack blinked and pretended to be fascinated with the wall.

"How about I do a set now and then I bet I get one more in before I knock off?" Brody asked.

Zack grinned. "Okay, then. Show me."

Brody did exactly that.

Despite remaining prickly the entire time, Brody worked his friggin' ass off. He did a few extras on top of each set, and he'd obviously done some PT at home. Dedicated and hardworking. Zack could respect that, and it made it hard not to admire the guy. Even when he was an asshole.

"I think I deserve another water for that." Brody panted, nodding toward the minifridge.

"I'll do you one better, Rocky. I've got Gatorade." He hopped up and grabbed two lemon-limes out of the fridge.

"Rocky?" Brody wrinkled his eyebrows. "What's that mean?"

"You know. Rocky Balboa, the—"

"Yeah, I know *who* Rocky is." He cut his eyes at Zack. "I mean what's with calling me Rocky?"

"Sorry, did I oh-fend?" Zack sat on the bench too.

"No."

"I just meant, y'know, Rocky was hard core. Didn't quit even if it kicked his ass in the process. You're attacking your PT like that. It's a good thing. Plus you've got the dark hair and all." He shrugged. "I don't know. Just came up with Rocky. I nickname everyone. Nothing personal."

Brody stared at him blank-faced.

He wasn't sure if Brody was about to laugh or punch him.

"Rocky's fine," Brody finally said, face still expressionless. "Bullwinkle."

Zack's burst of laughter bounced off the walls. "No, you didn't. I wasn't talking about *that* Rocky."

It was Brody's turn to shrug. "You've got the brown hair and all, long moose-like limbs." He flailed his arms around, managing to keep his face completely expressionless, not even the smallest smile.

Zack was going to hurt himself laughing. "Fine, fine. Fair enough. I'm a moose. I've been called worse."

Brody finally broke, and the faintest grin ghosted over his face. More like a curl of the lips. "Call 'em like I see 'em. But I like to think I'm a little better-looking than Stallone."

Zack had absolutely no comment on that whatsoever. Nope.

Brody was a dangerous combo, and Zack found himself wishing the man was hideous, a slouch, or at least a humorless tool bag. A whiney quitter with a bad 'tude was better than this complicated, driven, hotter-than-seven-hells cop with a wit so dry it was a fire hazard. He hadn't been this way with Matt, but for whatever reason, now something was alive inside Detective Brody.

Physically attractive was one thing. Zack saw good-looking men every day, and, while awesome to look at, it wasn't everything. A hot bod, even one like Brody's, wasn't unusual in his line of work or out on the beach. But attractive *and* dedicated? Unexpectedly funny and dedicated to his work?

Brody was a potent and dangerous drink. And as Zack sat close enough to know the smell of Brody's sweat and cologne, the long swallows of Gatorade making his thick neck move in a sinful arch, he knew he was about to fall off the wagon.

Chapter Four

Brody woke up with every muscle in his body hurting. "Sonuvabitch." He rolled to his side. He didn't even know he had muscles in some of these places. And he used to work out!

That was what happened when you were sedentary for months and then went at it like a pit bull, the way he had yesterday. He hadn't done it to impress his physical therapist either; he'd done it for himself.

Brody groaned as he sat up. Fucking Zack the PT from hell. Or heaven. Likely both.

He should've stuck with Matt. At least Matt was so obnoxious as to never distract him from what mattered, and he'd never stir any feeling besides derision and *Kill!*

No. That wouldn't do either. He hadn't been getting anywhere with Matt's lazy-ass methods, but now he was making progress. If he kept working at therapy like this, even if he had to endure Zack's long limbs, the high, round ass in those khakis, and that ridiculous mop of thick, shiny brown hair, he would be up and running soon.

The rigid stir in his boxers at the thought of any part of Zack made him want to punch something.

Oh, he was up all right.

"Bastard." Brody scooted to the edge of the bed and grabbed his crutches. He wasn't sure who was the bastard: him or Zack. Him for not being able to block Zack out—after all, he'd been blocking shit out for years, he ought to be a pro by now—or Zack for wheedling his way in with that big, unapologetic smile and boisterous laugh.

What the hell was up with that anyway? No one ever found Brody that funny, not even Lamont. He didn't want to like making Zack double over with laughter either.

"Ah, to hell with it." Brody made his way up and crutched into the bathroom. He managed to take a piss, get into the shower about as awkwardly as humanly possible, and get halfway through washing his hair without thinking of Zack again.

It wasn't until he ran his hands through his own hair, rinsing out the rosemary-scented suds, that Zack popped up uninvited.

Imagine washing and rinsing all that hair. It'd probably feel like silk between his fingers. It was a trite notion but no less true. It looked like silk. Honey brown, the perfect length to curl around his fingers, fist in his hand while that hot, avid mouth took him in all the way. The brush of his tongue along the length of Brody's cock.

Brody knew he'd gone from rinsing his hair to fisting his own dick, but he couldn't stop. He needed this. It'd been weeks now, since the surgery, and his body wanted the attention and release.

It'd been too long since he'd actually been with another person. Who was it last? There was the guy in Georgia, but that was in the spring. The bar girl in North Charleston. A quick blowjob in his car after last call. Dark and half-drunk, he could imagine anyone—which always worked best if he was with a woman. A mouth was a mouth was a mouth. Before that...oh yeah. It'd been a couple of months prior. In Tallahassee while doing some continuing ed work with the local PD.

Who knew Tallahassee had a big gay scene? Well, they did. And Brody was drawn to it like a fly to honey.

Two hours of arguing, telling himself not to go. His rental car veered right into the parking lot of The Castle, where he'd met the hottest redhead he'd ever seen in his life. Hot and about ten years his junior. Fuck it, the guy was stacked, and he'd made all the moves. That was good because Brody didn't make moves. He didn't even have moves. He'd ordered tequila and sat there. Red did the rest.

Small talk, but all the while, he was fucking Brody with his eyes. Telling him without words exactly all the things he'd let Brody do. Or do to Brody. He wasn't about to go that far, but fifteen minutes later they were in the bathroom, pants around his ankles while Red moaned and sucked, moaned and sucked.

He mimicked the motion now, the slick of the shampoo suds making it so easy.

He would picture Red with his sprinkling of freckles and light eyes. Thick fingers that grabbed and squeezed at his thighs. He would not picture smooth, tan skin, thick brown hair, and big brown eyes to match. Long, strong fingers that he knew could take him apart, stroke by capable stroke.

"Oh God." Brody felt the tightening in his balls at the slightest attention on Zack's image.

He couldn't. He couldn't give in and imagine that man on his knees. Worse yet he could not imagine himself on his knees, giving in to Zack. Bending to his will. He had to see Zack again, he had to be able to look the man in the face.

"Fuuuuuck," he growled, fisting himself hard, stroking faster.

No. He would picture the guy from the bar. Any of the other guys from any bar in any other state, but not Zack. Not someone he had to see again and again. Someone who might know, might figure it out, might threaten the walls so willfully constructed.

Brody forced the image of Red back into his mind. The picture was hazy, dull at best. His passion wavered and his dick softened. It pouted because Brody took away its new favorite image.

"No," he told himself. He was not going to have a jerk-off fantasy about his PT. Hell no.

Hell yes! his libido roared.

Brody bumped his head against the tile of his shower, three taps. Maybe he could rattle the sense back into his head. Shake the monkey of wanting men off his back. Why? Why did it have to be men?

Because they're fucking hot! came the answer.

He'd tried. Growing up in a house where it was clear as well-cleaned glass what was thought about men who dig other men, he'd tried like hell to be into women. Sometimes it even worked; sometimes it failed miserably with nothing but embarrassment. But he'd known. Even then. He'd always known.

"Fuck!" Brody glared at his fingers wrapped around his dick, the head of it red and crying for more.

It had to be men, and Brody hated himself for not being able to control that. He hated that he was taught to hate himself and anyone like him before he'd ever understood who he was. If not, maybe he wouldn't be so fucked-up right now. So fucked-up that nothing worked except men.

Works for me. Zack's words bounced back into his head.

Of course it did. Life probably came easy to Zack. Carefree, sunny smiles, and easy laughter.

Brody wanted to hate him for it. He wanted to be able to erase Zack from his mind because of some huge fault in his personality, work ethic, morals, or anything. But he couldn't. Zack probably had faults, but if he did, they weren't anywhere near the size of his own.

Zack would be a warm breeze in an otherwise frigid life.

What the hell was he thinking? He didn't even know if the man was gay. Even if he was, it didn't matter, because nothing would ever happen.

Never. Going. To. Happen.

Brody slapped the tiles with one hand and repositioned his fist with the other. He was focusing on Red, and that was it. Red and that black-and-white bathroom stall, the sounds of sucking and moaning, and the slippery tug on his dick.

Too bad the renewed focus did nothing for his dick.

The black and white kept swirling into professional gray. Gray carpet, light gray walls. Khaki pants and a white polo shirt, fit snug enough to drive him crazy. Tan arms, tan fingers holding his shoulder. Strong shoulder under his arm, keeping him from falling on his ass. The way those muscles felt beneath him, how they'd feel beneath his hungry fingers. How they'd feel looming over him, promising release. Deft hands unbuttoning his pants, slipping them down over his cheeks, his cock bobbing between them as Zack looked up at him, nothing but undisguised *want* in those perfect brown eyes.

"Fuck it!" Brody gave up the fight. He drew Zack to his mind, full and three-dimensional, all smiles and laughter, batting his brown eyes before he stripped Brody naked and promised to blow his world apart.

Zack chuckled, his breath heating Brody's dick as he used his mouth to nuzzle and taunt. Tease. Of course he'd be a tease; it fit his look perfectly. Dimples and a sinful mouth curling up as he licked his way along Brody's length and finally got down to business. Large hands cupped Brody's ass and drew him in.

He swore as Zack swallowed him down, sucking deep, eyes closed in pure bliss and Brody felt the rumble of satisfaction from Zack's throat as it vibrated deep into his balls. The slick heat had his knees buckling, hand scrambling for purchase and finding the breadth of Zack's shoulders. Zack was shirtless and Brody's fingers dug into the cut muscles of his shoulders. Tanned from the beach, tanned like the rest of him, eyes flashing as he looked up and took Brody in deeper.

Artful fingers ran up Brody's thigh to cup his balls and give them a gentle tug. Brody tensed with his building orgasm. The bolt of pleasure rushed down his chest and into his dick with the out-of-control power of a train off the tracks. With a groan, he had to reclaim his footing or he'd fall. He imagined sliding his hands up Zack's neck, into that mop of brown hair.

It *was* as silky as it looked. He knew it. And when Brody tugged, he thrust harder into Zack's mouth. The man only groaned in acceptance and dug his fingers deeper into the muscle of Brody's ass.

Brody lost it. He came so damn hard he curled in on himself with the power of it. Pumping long into Zack's wet mouth, releasing a drawn-out moan and panting as his chest heaved with the release.

As soon as Brody managed to switch his brain back on and look down, his image of Zack was grinning up at him, deep brown eyes glinting, oh so pleased with himself and looking at Brody to return the favor.

Brody wanted to do exactly that. He wanted to see and hear

the real Zack fall apart *and* be the reason why. That realization threw him headfirst back into reality.

Zack's warm brown eyes turned into the bland white of Brody's bathroom tiles. His release gave way to the rushing water of the shower. The dark mess of his mind barreled back front and center. The high of endorphins disappeared, replaced with self-loathing. Brody dropped his head back against the tiles and cursed himself. He thumped the tiles with his hand and let the feelings wash over him until the warm water ran cold and chilled him to his core.

He was *not* going to do this. There was no way any of what he'd just imagined would ever happen. Even if possible, he couldn't allow it. He wouldn't.

His father would turn in his grave; his coworkers would turn their backs on him. Deadly denial for a cop. He'd buried that part of himself for so long, it'd warped him. He could control it, he'd done so for years, and no pretty PT boy was going to screw his head up even further. Brody had a life and a career that needed him. He'd found a routine that worked, and he would not sacrifice it for passing sexual pleasure.

No. Hell no. He could go on living as he'd lived his whole life. It suited him just fine, and it worked. And if being buddy-buddy with Zack was a threat to that, then to hell with him. No more joking, no more small talk, no more nicknames, and definitely no more fantasizing. If Zack didn't get the hint from cool disregard, then Brody had years of practice at being a complete asshole.

It shouldn't take much to make Zack step off.

Chapter Five

Brody was mega-pissed; that much was obvious.

Zack was already accustomed to the fluctuating moods, ranging from withdrawn and icy to *almost* amused, but now there was a seething rage he took out on the innocent equipment.

Zack felt bad for the poor weights as they were again clunked down on the last rep.

"Easy on the metal," he muttered.

Brody ignored him, wiping his forehead with a towel and reaching down to grab his crutches.

He launched himself into the next exercise, ran through the minimum, and threw himself into the reps. Then he was on to the next, glancing up at the clock for the bazillionth time. It'd been like this all day. So unlike him not to add in extra reps or accept Zack's subtle challenge to push himself a step further. Brody had a fire on his ass making him rush through, sloppy and ineffective.

And if he thought Zack would keep letting it fly, especially when he could injure himself even worse, he had another think coming.

"Hey." Zack tried interrupting him.

It did nothing.

"Hey!" Zack pushed at Brody's shoulder and had him sitting back down on the machine. "Hold up a sec."

The flinch was there, but Zack ignored it. He reached for Brody's leg and elevated it, touching around the healing scar, noting the swelling. He lifted it farther, and Brody stretched into it. Good to see he at least cooperated that much.

Still holding the leg up, Zack pulled the water bottle out of his pocket and handed it to Brody. "We're going to move on to stretches and ROM exercises. We've done enough weights for today."

Brody frowned, and Zack could see the protest building.

"We usually spend longer on weights. Why stop?" His tone was clipped and cool.

Zack wasn't about to tell him that he'd hit them hard enough already and this was a covert attempt to move him away before he hurt himself. Saying that to a man like Brody was waving the red cape for a bull.

"Yeah, just trying to mix it up. Keep your body guessing." Zack kept his voice light as he held out his hand to retrieve the bottled water. "Let's do a couple of stretches for range of motion. We did them last week."

Brody frowned as he got to his feet. Then he didn't move from where he hung off the crutches, knuckles tensing on the grips.

Zack took a deep breath and tried to meet Brody's eyes. No such luck as Brody kept them on the mat, their steel gray boring holes all the way through the floor.

"Do you remember the—"

"I remember the fucking stretches." It came out as a blasted snarl.

Zack crossed his arms. "Okay. What's the problem?"

"The problem is this is bullshit." Brody met his gaze, now boring a hole through him. "I should be strengthening. I need to be stronger. I've got shit to *do*."

"Oh *really?*" Zack didn't budge. Who did this guy think he was? He'd felt like maybe they were heading toward some kind of successful therapeutic relationship. Now, not only was he getting shut out again, he was being told how to do his job?

Clearly Brody hadn't met Zack's pit bull side.

Being passive and refusing to rise to Brody's bait hadn't worked for long; being a nice guy hadn't worked. Time to meet Brody on his terms.

"I want to see you do a couple of reps of this *shit* first. Then we'll ice your knee and call it a day before you tear it up again."

Brody didn't back down either. Zack hadn't expected him to, but even hobbling on crutches, the man managed to intimidate. The shoulders hunched over were still just as broad and the glare was no less scary.

Zack was suddenly glad he had a clean driving history and no parking tickets.

Brody moved closer. "I said I was done with the monkey tricks. I want to do something that'll actually get me off these fucking things." He used his weight and height to get in Zack's space.

Problem was Zack was still taller and hadn't been scared of bullies since his growth spurt at sixteen. He stepped in as well, coming up close enough to see the steel in Brody's gaze.

"Do you want to get better, or do you want to drive a desk for the next thirty years?"

The look Brody gave him was a combo of eat-shit-and-die and are-you-even-speaking-English?

Zack repeated the question.

"I want to get better," Brody snarled. "Of course I fucking do."

"Then you will listen to *me*. Not just your drive, not your ego, and not your ever-present pride. *Me*. I said I'd get you to department code, and I will. Hell, I can get you beyond code, but you have to stop fighting me at every turn. You *will* slow down when I say you're pushing it too hard. You'll do it *before* you undo everything we've accomplished. I accept that you're probably top dog out there on the police force, but you need to accept that I'm top dog in here. I know what the hell I'm talking about, so how about you shut up, listen up, and do what I say?"

Brody's glare turned to eyes as round as quarters before narrowing again as he contemplated the gauntlet Zack threw down.

Zack wasn't surprised. He'd bet his damn degree that Brody never expected him to raise his voice *and* get in his face. They logged in a thirty-second stare-off before Brody finally nodded. Zack could've sworn he saw a flicker of respect cross Brody's hard features before it disappeared.

"Fine," Brody bit off.

It wasn't until Zack felt the huff of breath brush his cheeks that he realized they stood entirely too close.

Their proximity and the heat from the argument caused a different kind of tension to rise. Zack felt his squashed attraction for the man sprout anew and grow even stronger. He liked someone who wasn't scared to go toe-to-toe with him. Right now, Brody looked ready to battle, crutches be damned. Zack stepped back and gave a short wave to the mat. "Then let's see it." Brody hobbled over, shoving the crutches at him before he began the exercises.

The rest of the session flowed, but Zack kept waiting for the other shoe to drop.

It never did.

Brody did the stretches. He cooperated as Zack took him through basic range of motion and finally directed him to the back room to elevate his leg and ice down.

Yes, he continued to scowl like the entire world offended him by its very existence, but Zack could handle that. He was pretty sure it was Brody's neutral gear anyway. He'd fall backward on his ass if Brody ever cracked a full, genuine smile.

After ten minutes, he checked on Brody in recovery. He was lying down, leg elevated and ice pack firmly in place. The arm slung over his eyes revealed the curve of his triceps perfectly.

Have mercy.

He rested the other on the flat of his stomach; a patch of skin showed above the waist of his basketball shorts, a line of dark hair delved lower still.

Zack swallowed and aimed the question at the spot on the gray wall above Brody's head. "How're we doing?"

Brody lifted his arm to look over. And, of course, scowl. "Don't know how *we* are doing, but my knee hurts like a bitch."

Maybe this was all nature's way of making it possible to interact with the man on a professional level. Take a man *so* damn sexy, fuckable, and determined, but then toss in the fact he was the biggest ass so that everyone didn't fall all over him at every interaction.

Pity the being-an-ass thing didn't put Zack off. Hell, it only made him more of a challenge, and Zack was all about conquering the impossible. He shook his head and walked over to examine Brody's knee.

Brody was a patient. Off-limits. Business. Professional. *Focus.*

He removed the ice. There was swelling but nothing unexpected. He lifted the ankle, keeping his hand on the knee joint, feeling as it moved smoothly.

He stopped when Brody tensed. No show of bitching, though, just a hardening of the jaw, stiffened shoulders as he let Zack move his leg. Zack lowered the leg back down and replaced the ice pack. "I think you'll live."

Brody's shoulders relaxed, but he still grumbled, "Maybe. No thanks to you."

It sounded like the pouting of a petulant child, but it was coming from such a large, full-grown man, Zack couldn't help the laugh that bubbled out.

Brody raised an eyebrow as Zack continued to chuckle, shaking his head. "I thought cops were supposed to be tough."

Brody's answer to that was a look that surely scared most people shitless.

Zack wasn't most people.

The scowl, the intensity of those gray eyes—the guy *needed* to lighten up. They'd hit a bump in the road today but managed. He wasn't about to let Brody go back to being the difficult patient he had been at the start. Life was too short for all this damn drama, and right now, they needed a laugh.

Zack leaned over Brody and grabbed the stethoscope hanging on the wall next to the blood pressure cuff.

"What are you doing?" Brody eyed him, following every movement.

Zack continued to angle the headset. He placed the tips in his ears and leaned over, then put the diaphragm to Brody's chest. "Making sure you'll live."

The corner of Brody's mouth quirked as he fought off a

smirk. He muttered something and shoved at Zack's hands. "Man...get off me."

Amusement lit his eyes, so Zack continued, putting his serious doctor face on—which was bullshit, because he couldn't stop grinning.

"I really should check. I may have done you in, what with your delicate health and all. I won't know unless I find a heartbeat," Zack said.

Brody continued to shove, even as he fought harder and harder not to smile. Zack did laugh as Brody finally shook his head, rolled his eyes, and lowered his hands in defeat. "Fine. Make sure I'll live." He looked Zack in the eyes and added, "Smart-ass."

Zack continued to listen to the steady beat and grinned as Brody rolled his eyes to heaven.

He could even work out a resting heart rate from this, listening to the strong thumps, quickly glancing down at his watch. Decent. Resting below sixty. Brody was fit. A lot more fit than he gave himself credit for. The muscles in his chest were defined, and that didn't come from police work. He had to work out regularly.

The meat of Zack's hand rested on his broad chest, fingers moving on the swell of his pectorals as they rose and fell with each breath. The stir in his shorts brought him back front and center to the fact that this wasn't the best idea. Leaning over his very attractive and touch-phobic patient. Even if all he intended to do was see if the man could lighten up. Maybe even laugh.

He wasn't laughing now. When Zack lifted his eyes to Brody's, he was hit with the full intensity of stormy gray. Not filled with amusement anymore but with something else.

It sent heat down Zack's spine and into his shoes. He wasn't even listening to the beats, just frozen in place with the buds in his ears, fingers still pressed to Brody's chest as they stared at each other. The humor of the moment fell away as Brody continued to stare, arms still folded behind his head, mouth set into a straight line.

Zack straightened a tad too sharply and tucked the scope around his neck. Pulling his face into a rehearsed, easy smile, he hid the heat thrumming in his veins. "Yeah. You'll live." He started backing toward the door and gave a lame salute that made him want to cringe. God he was such a spaz. "I...I'll see you next week, Rocky."

He rushed to exit stage left, narrowly missing the doorframe on the way out.

Chapter Six

Two weeks. Two weeks down and only thirty more minutes remaining. One last session and Zack would be done dealing with Detective Douglas Brody.

Not that Brody was the issue anymore. The opposite, actually. Brody showed up and did what Zack told him. Even now he practiced knee bends, sans crutches, on top of the balance trainer. He wasn't overly friendly or warm and fuzzy during their hour, but he wasn't a tool bag anymore either. He got down to business and stayed focused. He'd made tremendous progress as a result, and today he'd be checked off as ready for light duty.

No, Brody wasn't the problem at all. Zack was.

Every session, every time they had small talk in the last ten minutes before he left, Zack felt a now familiar gravitational pull toward the man. In those last ten minutes, he didn't want Brody to go. As much as he knew Brody needed to go, for sanity's sake, he wanted him to stay. He wanted to know more. Crack that tough exterior, have a couple of beers together…maybe grope one of those massive thighs to feel it tense beneath his palm.

"Get a grip," Zack muttered to himself and made busy writing notes for Brody's file. The man either wasn't gay or, if he was, he was so latent he may as well be dead. Regardless, in a few minutes he wouldn't be in Zack's life anymore. Gone. Thanks for the help. And Zack could get back to reality and focus his energy on a good-looking, gay, *friendly* guy who was into him.

Shit. At what age would he grow out of the unrequited longing for some hot-as-hell straight guy who would freak out at the notion of even touching another man?

Maybe his next birthday.

"What next, Doc?" Brody asked, stepping off the half ball.

Oh, and that. He'd taken to calling Zack "Doc" ever since the joke with the stethoscope. The day Zack had been sure he'd given himself away and Brody was going to show up the next time and beat his ass. But Brody had left that day like nothing happened and showed up every session after like nothing was amiss. No biggie. Other than calling him Doc and Moose from time to time.

"Let's try some knee curls. Easy on the weight, higher reps." Zack notched the weight at forty-five pounds, and Brody pumped away, no questions asked, sweat making his skin slick. Skin that would be hot to the touch and smooth under his fingers.

See? There he went again.

"I'll be back in a sec," Zack called, stepping over to one of the empty desks. He could trust Brody to do his reps properly now, and he needed to get away. If not, there was the distinct possibility he'd end up openly ogling Brody's sculpted legs and then licking his chops like a hungry tiger.

Yeah, that'd go over *so* well.

His mind was made up. Tonight, after he finished here, Zack would go to the party his friend kept talking about. He'd go and he'd meet a guy and at least date someone with a snowball's chance of a future. Hardened, cynical, smoking-hot cops were not in his life plan. Not if he wanted to maintain any sanity or chance of emotional health.

Brody pumped away on the machine in the background, and Zack focused on his notes and file work. Soon they'd be finished. He'd shake hands with Brody, and that would be it. No more awkward moments of silence, no more avoiding looking at the man for fear of getting caught. Zack could get on with everyday, normal work. Get on with life, not thinking about the next time Brody came to see him. No more cracking jokes just to see Brody smirk. No more busting out with a laugh on the rare occasions Brody made a funny. No more Moose, no more Rocky. Back to real life. And it was about damn time.

"All done, Doc. What's next?"

Zack looked up at Brody's set gaze. No more seeing him

twice a week. No more seeing him again. Ever.

Damn.

"That's it, man," Zack said. "You're done. Just icing down and then you're free to go."

"Really?" Brody looked at his watch like someone had just told him it was time to go skydiving. "Time flies when you can finally walk on two feet again."

Yes, it did.

Zack set Brody up with the ice, and, just like every other session for the last two weeks even though he swore he wouldn't, he checked on him with the last ten minutes remaining.

"Feeling pretty good?" Zack asked.

"Damn sight better than a month and a half ago, that's for sure." Brody turned to look at him, arm thrown up like always, same patch of skin showing just above his shorts.

"Good." Zack nodded. "I hate to say I told you so, but—"

Brody laughed. A full-bodied, openmouthed smile that caught Zack so off guard he almost fell from his leaning spot against the wall.

"No, you *don't!*" Brody shook his head as their eyes locked. "You fucking love getting to say I told you so. Go ahead, then"—he waved Zack on—"get it out of your system."

Zack straightened himself, still reeling from Brody's laughter. "Uh... I told you so?" He tried again. "I told you so. I *so* told you so."

"Don't get carried away." Brody turned his gaze to the ceiling.

Zack didn't want to grin, but he felt himself smiling from ear to ear. He'd taken the toughest patient he'd ever met and gotten him back in working shape. Not only that, he'd made the man laugh. Damn. He was going to miss this. The hotness, yeah, but also...this. Underneath all that hard, sharp exterior was a likable guy. He'd never tell Brody that, but still. Their banter. Their interaction. The chemistry. It couldn't *all* be in his head. They...meshed.

Shit. If he had any sense of self-preservation, it was past time to get away from the man.

"So look," Brody said, pushing to sit up, keeping the ice in place with one hand. "Remember when I pissed you off?"

Zack couldn't resist. "You'll have to be more specific."

"Ha-ha. Okay. Remember when I pissed you off enough for you to go Billy Bad Ass on me and you were all 'This is *my* house, these are my rules'?"

Zack quirked his lips and shook his head. "Pretty sure that's not what I said. Same point, but I'd never say *These are my rules*."

"Whatever. Point is, you said you could do more than get me up to code. You said you could get me beyond code. What did you mean by that?"

Zack's stomach plummeted. Crap, crap, *crap*. He'd meant, given a little more time, he could have Brody in the best shape of his life. But that was just talk. That was before he'd realized he should never hang around Brody like they could be buddies. They could *never* be buddies.

"Hello? Was that just angry ranting or what?" Brody raised both eyebrows, his typical impatience rearing up.

Zack knew there would be no getting out of this conversation. "No, I meant, if you really wanted to get back to where you were before, or beyond, it'll take more than a few weeks of PT. It'll take daily focus with...y'know..."

Brody raised both eyebrows and waited. Obviously he didn't know.

"A trainer," Zack blurted. "You can work with a trainer and get into the kind of condition that'd rival any athlete. You have the genetics. Join a gym or—"

"I don't do gyms. Detective hours don't work with a gym. I have weights at home."

Zack just bet he did. "Cool; then that's a start."

"So just go back to lifting weights like I did before, and I'll kick our physical testing standards in the balls?" He didn't sound convinced.

With good reason. The physical therapist in Zack was raging at him to do the right thing here. If a patient needed help, it was his duty to help. His fitness-buff side was appalled that he might not speak up and help Brody out, even as the rest of him knew he needed to get far, far away.

"No," Zack admitted. "Not really." *Damn, damn, damn.* "You need a trainer to do it safely and properly yet push you to the next level." *Don't ask me, don't ask me, do not ask me.*

"You're the only physical therapist I know. How much?"

"Huh?" He blinked at Brody. How had he gotten here? After today, he was supposed to be safe. And on top of all that, he was *so* full of shit. He couldn't claim he wasn't jumping at the chance to train with Brody, stay in his life a little while longer even if it meant torture for another month or two.

"How much to be my personal trainer?"

"I don't know. I've never done professional training outside of here," Zack hedged. "I don't even know that I can. I'll have to check, but it's probably against company policy."

"Then don't tell anyone." Brody shrugged like that was a no-brainer. "Bend the rules; don't break them. Whatever the cost, I want you as my trainer. You know what you're doing, just do it for another month or two."

Zack knew what it felt like to get asked out by a man. He'd been asked out plenty. Unfortunately, that wasn't what this was. This was a cop wanting to get back on his job ASAP, and he saw Zack as the only way to get there.

"I've got maybe another month to six weeks before I test for full active duty." Brody kept going. "I need to knock my captain into the next county with my PT. *You* can make that happen. You have to get me ready. I don't care about the cost. Deal?"

He was insane for even considering this. Certifiable. No one should want to work with Brody based on mood swings alone, never mind it being the gay physical therapist working with the guy who was hotter than any porn-star cop in any adult movie. Was he a sadist?

"Okay. Deal." Zack took Brody's offered hand. Warm and solid. Self-assured and oozing intense sex appeal, just like the rest of him.

Zack could hear Beethoven playing his Funeral March even as they shook on it.

—�֎—

Brody watched Zack hop in place next to a dark green 4Runner as he pulled into the parking spot next to him. Zack's hands were stuffed in a gray hoodie, a baseball cap covering most of his face.

Early as usual. The guy had a thing about showing up long before being "on time."

He looked up as Brody opened the car door, big smile on his face. How could anyone buzz around like a bumblebee on crack at this hour? Brody felt every muscle as he pulled out of bed this morning.

Sure, Zack delivered on every damn promise, and Brody was up and running again—well, slowly running—but early mornings still caused his knee to ache like a bitch. He accepted the ache with a wave of gratitude. He was off crutches. He'd be back on active soon.

Zack would never know what it meant that he was helping Brody even further, getting him more than just capable of duty. The job was everything, and the prospect of going back to Homicide, back to his calling, stronger than ever, it made him want to wrap his arms around Zack—mostly with gratitude, maybe also a heavy dose of something else.

But he wouldn't.

Brody rubbed over the Velcro as he walked over. Zack opened his driver-side door, took off his cap, and threw it onto the seat. Ridiculous. He didn't even have abysmal hat hair. It was still damp, the silk curling perfectly at the ends.

"You find it okay?" he asked.

Brody folded his arms and leaned against his Charger as he watched Zack tug at his hoodie. "I've been here before."

"Oh yeah? Good."

Zack pulled the thin sweatshirt over his head, and Brody cursed to himself as the shirt rode up and his gaze fell to the dip at Zack's hip.

Yes, that golden skin was *everywhere*. Only a hint of paler skin peeked out from the low waist of his shorts. *Fuck.* He didn't need to know any of this, but he sure as shit didn't look away.

He'd managed to keep his lust tempered for the last month with only one or two more shower moments that featured Zack in the starring role. This was pushing it, but he'd suffer through not only to get back on the job but get back to being the *best* on the job.

"At least you'll know the trail if you know the area, right? Don't have to worry about losing you if you fall behind." Zack stretched his long legs as he led the way to the bike path.

Brody cut his eyes over. "Yeah. I shot a guy just up there last year, so I know the area pretty well."

"Holy shit! For real?" Zack's reaction was priceless. His eyes bugged out from beneath a floppy fall of his hair, and his mouth dropped open. The comical expression distracted Brody's brain just enough to keep him from plunging into another crappy episode of self-punishment.

Zack's facial expressions ran through a supermarket of emotions before Brody cracked in amusement and a grin slipped out.

"You're lying?" Zack gaped. "Oh my God, you're a dick for lying about that."

Brody let out a huff of a laugh, and Zack shoved at his shoulder with a full smile.

"Who lies about shooting someone?"

"Cop humor." Brody shrugged.

"Nice. Must be a real riot down at the station." Zack pulled a face. "Fah-reeeaks!"

He had no argument there. All homicide detectives were a little different. They had to be in order to cope. There were inside jokes in their department they could never utter to the civilian world.

"All right, look it." Zack stopped at the side of the path and pulled one leg up behind him to stretch it.

Brody refused to look and instead focused on his face, which wasn't a huge help.

"We're going to do a mile and see how it goes first. We'll take it easy." He stretched out the emphasis on easy, the word pulling at his full lips.

Brody was sick to death of taking it easy. He'd been taking it easy on crutches for months, but Zack knew what he was doing, so he wasn't going to bitch. Much.

As they started at a slow jog, Zack gave a little chuckle, shaking his head.

"What?"

Zack looked over and gave Brody a full-force Zack-grin, brown eyes sparkling. "I can't believe you joked about shooting someone, but there are two things I can't believe more than that. One, that you cracked a joke. Two, after all this time, you haven't learned *not* to give your trainer crap. Payback is hell on the legs, y'know?"

He shrugged and kept pace. There was a lot of shit he hadn't learned not to do, regardless of how bad it turned out for him.

They didn't say much during the jog, and when they reached the one-mile marker, Zack ran in place, knees high, as he did some kind of mobile patient assessment.

"How're you doing? How's the knee?"

Fucker wasn't even winded. "Doing okay." Brody refused to breathe any way but normally. "I could do more."

"You sure?" Zack did more visual analysis and looked doubtful.

"Yeah, I'm fucking sure," he snapped, and then bit it back when Zack's gaze jerked to his. He wasn't pissed at Zack, just old habit. He wasn't the poor SOB on crutches anymore, and he couldn't stand for anyone, especially Zack, to treat him like he was. He should maybe apologize, but he couldn't bring himself to—

"Nah, you're right." Zack didn't give him the chance, like he knew the twisted trail of his mind. "You should be well able to knock out a mile by now, or I'm a shitty PT. Let's do another and see what's what."

They jogged another mile, at a quicker pace, but not so much as to be too noticeable. When Brody didn't complain, they kept going. At the start of the third mile, Zack began with the chitchat.

Yeah, the guy liked to talk. Loved to talk, actually, but he knew Zack was also gauging his ability to hold a small convo while running. Any panting, gasping, or groaning in pain would end their run faster than a summertime downpour.

"So, seriously…" Zack started. "You come out to the park to jog before? Bike?"

He remembered all the times he'd been to this park on business when on patrol. People didn't want to know about the seedy side of anything. Not really. But Zack asked, so…

"I did my rookie year with the county when I got out of the academy," he told him. "Our car covered this area, and sometimes we'd get calls. No, I never shot anyone," he added when Zack shot him a look. "The park is pretty safe. Some drunk and disorderly. A few run-of-the-mill pervs we'd have to haul in. All pretty standard."

"Uhm… Sick." Zack glanced behind a tree as they passed it. "Like…streakers? Peeping Toms? What?"

"You name it." Brody shrugged. "Lots of indecent exposure. Guys driving around with no pants on. Stop and ask the female joggers for directions."

"You're lying!" Zack exclaimed.

Brody glanced at him as they ran on. "You don't get out much, do you?"

Zack scowled. It was criminal in its sex appeal. "I get out. Just, y'know, not much pervy happens around the clinic."

He'd be surprised. Unpleasantly shocked, more like. But that was part of Brody's job too. He dealt with the ugly shit so good citizens like Zack didn't have to.

"I bet not much happens in your neighborhood either." Brody smirked. "Big gated thing, I bet. All white, all the time. Everyone drives a Beemer."

"Screw you." Zack veered toward him, making him run over in the wet grass. Zack grinned as he cussed. "I happen to live out on Folly, thanks s'much. Surfers and hippies and not a Beemer in sight."

"Oh, look at you. Up with people," he taunted, then bit the inside of his mouth. He did not need to start that. Zack wasn't someone he should joke around with and tease. Teasing and Zack brought on imagery of a whole different scenario.

Brody thought about his last crime scene. Anything to get rid of Zack's image. Made it difficult when Zack ran right beside him and was now laughing.

"Man, screw you. Like you don't live in the suburbs?"

"I live here, on the island. In a condo. Not the suburbs."

"The whole island *is* the suburbs!" Zack chuckled. "But you live over here? Really?"

Brody nodded. Yes. He lived close. Close enough to have Zack over for a beer. Which wouldn't happen.

"I love it here." Zack kept chatting, and he was grateful for the chance to think of something else.

How was he ever going to be able to make this work? Zack was a great PT, and he had no doubt the guy could get him in the kind of shape that'd blow the physical assessment out of the water, but at what cost? Maybe if he just didn't respond. He could let Zack ramble on but not contribute. Refuse to let the chitchat equal them getting to know each other and becoming buddies.

Ramble on Zack did. On and on. About how much he liked jogging, how well Brody was doing, how this was the perfect track for now and how they could ramp up to something that challenged him further. He went over his plan to basically make Brody the most athletic detective on the force. Then he started in on the Charleston weather, the beach.

"I know!" He got a little louder. "Next session, let's hit the beach. The sand offers natural resistance..." He went silent as he seemed to think to himself.

Brody wondered what could possibly be going on in that busy brain, when Zack piped up again.

"It'll be perfect. Lunges, even walking will use more muscle and effort. Perfect. Okay, so next time we'll meet near the pier. I think we give it a couple of days' recovery, be sure to stretch in between, and then we can meet at this same time on Thursday. Plenty of parking this early; we'll jog on the beach and then go into resistance. Yeah, it will be awesome."

His excitement was obvious, but Brody refused to let it be endearing. Zack's dedication to his job, to getting Brody fully up to speed, meant a lot. He just couldn't let it mean too much.

And it was more than a little funny that not once, in the last fifteen minutes, had Brody's input been necessary in any way.

"Three miles, man," Zack said, pointing to the marker as they rounded a turn and could see their cars in the distance. "Not too shabby for an invalid." He used Brody's words against him.

Brody flipped him the bird.

Zack's response was to laugh. Of course.

Laugh at this, Brody thought, and bumped his speed up a notch. Invalid his ass. He was not going to be seen as such. Beside him, Zack matched the increase.

Brody smirked and ran a little faster. Without a word, Zack matched it and then some. He pulled ahead a few paces and Brody kicked it into fourth gear. By the time they reached the cars, they were running wide open, Zack and his long-ass legs beating him by about four feet.

"Sonuvabitch." Brody panted as he jogged to a stop.

"Walk it," Zack told him. "Don't stop. Keep it moving."

Thank God Zack was at least a little winded too; otherwise, Brody might punch him. They walked along the path, Zack with a smile like he'd just won a marathon, Brody wondering what had possessed him to show off. He'd pay for it tomorrow, while Zack wouldn't feel a thing.

"Ballsy move trying to race me," Zack said, still grinning. "Gotta hand it to you, but you've got a ways to go before you catch a college track star." He thumbed his chest.

Brody made a show of rolling his eyes.

"Maybe in a few months, Detective." He kept digging.

"Few months. Fuck that. I'm outrunning your ass before then. Somehow. I'll just shoot you in the leg and jog on past if it comes to it."

Zack's laugh boomed around the park.

Brody shook his head but smiled at the sound anyway. Then the cramp hit him.

"Sonuvabitch," he said again, but this time he ground it out between clenched teeth as pain clamped down on his thigh like a fucking Rottweiler.

"What?" Zack went on instant therapist red alert. "What happened? Where's the pain?" His focus went right to Brody's left knee.

That wasn't the issue. It was his right thigh hurting like a motherfucker.

"Cramp," Brody ground out, and couldn't even make it to his car as he crumpled and leaned on Zack's bumper. He jabbed a finger toward the offending leg.

"Gotcha." Zack nodded. "Here, come over here. Easy. Easy." He led Brody over to the still-damp grass. "Charlie horse. Probably from favoring the right leg to go easy on the left knee. You can't do that."

Brody gave him a death glare. "Thanks for clearing that up, Doc."

"Lie down." Zack knelt with Brody's hand on his arm.

"Lie down?" The grass was cold and wet. Wet grass was not going to help his leg.

Again Zack seemed to read his mind. "You have to lie down to stretch it out properly. Grass that's a little damp or the hard concrete. Your choice."

Brody lowered himself down with a scowl.

"Good choice," Zack said. "On your back." He waited until Brody was situated, then took his right heel in one hand and pressed the palm of his other hand against the ball of the foot, the toes going skyward, then farther back.

"Ow! Sonuva*bitch*!" Brody shouted.

"Leave my momma out of this; she's a good woman." Zack grinned.

"Basta— Fucking sadist," Brody tried.

"That's more like it. Give it a minute." He pressed back on the foot again. "It'll release in a bit."

Didn't fucking feel like it. Brody dug his fingers into the grass and down into the dirt because he refused to whimper like a little girl. A second later he felt something let go inside his leg. The pain eased, but it didn't disappear. His face must've shown relief, because Zack shifted and moved a hand to his calf.

"Better?" he asked.

Brody managed a nod.

"Keep the foot flexed and loosen the leg." He tapped Brody on the thigh. "Loosen."

Zack could be downright pushy when he went into health-care-professional mode. Brody wasn't used to being told what to do. The small voice inside him that rejoiced in response was the one he hated most. He clenched his eyes shut and relaxed his leg.

"Good," Zack said, his voice low as he focused.

He scooted himself up, knelt down, and hooked Brody's knee over his arm, placing one hand at the back of his thigh, the other on the front. Brody tensed everywhere. He didn't mean to, he probably shouldn't, but he couldn't help it.

"Relax. Hey," Zack said, and didn't say another word until Brody opened his eyes and met Zack's gaze. "Relax. The cramp comes right back if you're tense. Trust me."

Brody nodded again because it was all he could manage. It wasn't that he didn't trust Zack. Oddly enough, he did. But he didn't trust himself. He didn't like being in someone else's hands—yet he did. He wasn't comfortable with the vulnerability, but he was. And the position he was in was more than a tad suggestive. Except, of course, to someone like Zack. Zack, who only saw physiology, muscles, and ice packs. Cramps instead of sexual tension. Charlie horses instead of thighs.

"Good," Zack repeated as Brody relaxed.

Brody focused on the trees to his left and tried not to think about the man between his legs or the hands all over him. It made him wonder about the next time he could get out of town.

"Is this helping?" Zack asked.

"Huh? Oh...yeah. Thanks," Brody answered without looking at him.

Zack didn't say anything. Didn't move. Didn't seem to breathe.

Brody knew it was his way of making Brody either talk or look at him or pay attention. Drove him fucking nuts, but it worked. Brody turned his head to glare at Zack like a pissed-off delinquent, but when his eyes found Zack, Zack wasn't looking back.

Zack's gaze was somewhere below Brody's waist, dragging along one thigh, then the other. His attention lingered there, and Brody felt it all the way through his skin. It wasn't professional Zack checking out his alignment either. Far from.

Something different, something hungry flashed in the deep brown of Zack's eyes. Brody felt a lick of pure heat drag up his spine and back down. Straight to his groin. He didn't know what he did to make Zack meet his eyes. He didn't flinch or gasp or do anything besides remain frozen in place. Still, Zack looked at him, his eyes weaving a tale that had *nothing* to do with physical therapy.

Grasping fingers, slick skin, entwined bodies, and the kind of intensity that hurt so good you'd want it again and again. It sparked between them and hung in the air, thicker than the midsummer humidity. Brody recognized the same lust that continued to torture him right there in Zack's eyes.

"Okay." Brody pushed himself to sit up and slid back. "I'm okay now. Much better."

Zack seemed to shake himself out of it. "You sure you're okay?"

"Yep. Okay. Doing great."

"Oh. Okay."

How many times could they both say the fucking word "okay."

Zack shook his head and pushed himself to stand up. Brody managed to get up before Zack could offer him a hand.

"Well..." Zack looked around like he wasn't sure where they were anymore. "Good run. It's a good start. So...the beach next time?"

"Yeah. The beach." Brody nodded, feeling like a damn bobblehead doll. "See you then. Thanks." He stuck his hand out to shake Zack's because he didn't know what else to do, but it'd be weird if they didn't. Though it was weird now that they did.

Zack shook it. "See you then."

With those three words, Brody spun on his heels and still-aching thigh and quick-stepped it to his Charger. He got in and pulled out of the parking lot in record time because he had to get away to think.

This was bad. Very bad. Potential catastrophe in the making. Because not only was he attracted to his physical therapist who he could never be with—but now, there was little denying Zack was attracted right back.

CHAPTER SEVEN

Zack wasn't sure which was more irritating: the sand in his shoes or that he continued to get lost in staring at Brody no matter how hard he tried to look at something else. Seagulls? Maniacal but not intriguing enough to hold his attention. The ocean? Gorgeous, but the call of the waves didn't drown out the voice in his head reminding him of their last time together.

They'd worked out in silence so far, except for Brody's bellyaching. What they weren't saying only told Zack he hadn't imagined the electricity between them. Brody on the ground beneath him, thick, strong legs surrounding him, storm-cloud eyes pulling Zack in, no doubt recognizing the same lust that was probably scrawled all over Zack's face.

Damn.

A gaggle of runners sprinted by. Zack tried watching them, focusing on their form and athleticism. Brody called him on it.

"Am I doing this right? I feel like a damn idiot. I don't do these at home for exactly this reason, so you better tell me if I'm about to pull something, because I don't know what the hell I'm doing."

He'd been like this since they began. Complaining more than usual, acting so much like the Brody he'd met two months ago. Zack's theory on why supported that Brody was just as unnerved by the other day as he was. But he wasn't going to test it.

"Let me see," Zack told him. "Turn around and do another set, back that way."

Brody grumbled under his breath as he turned, but he lunged away perfectly.

The truth was, at this point in his training, this should be a fairly easy workout. Brody's complaining didn't come from the difficulty of the exercise. It came from within. Zack wasn't an idiot, and he knew people. Something was bugging the shit out of Brody, but he wasn't the kind of guy you asked to have a heart-to-heart. Chat it out. Discuss feelings.

Another truth struck him too. He needed to never stand on *this* side of Brody's lunges; his ass and defined hamstrings pulled tight.

Hell no.

Zack jogged ahead and watched Brody come toward him. "That's good. You've got it," he assured him.

"Doesn't feel like I've got jack." Brody wobbled as he lunged deeper.

"Not too deep right now. We'll get to that later." Zack bit his lip as soon as he said it, those two sentences bringing up a whole other image besides lunges. Jeez, he was such a perv.

It was Brody's fault. The man caused sex on the brain. *A lot* of sex on the brain after the other day. That look. Zack's hands on those strong thighs, the heat rising between them. The recognition. The energy that crackled between them, the drawn-out seconds of *What the hell is this?*

Zack wasn't prone to hallucinations, and there was no way the sizzle and pop the last time they were together was all in his head. It wasn't all one-sided either. He knew what interest looked like. He couldn't call it downright lust, because Brody had blanked out on him faster than the speed of sound. But there had been a moment, as he touched Brody's skin, flesh against flesh, when Zack had seen honest acknowledgment in those gray eyes. Awareness. The awareness between one person and another as sexual beings. *Desirable* sexual beings.

What he was supposed to do with that information, he had no idea.

He realized he'd stopped dead in the middle of Brody's path through the deep sand when he groaned out of the last lunge.

"Okay." Brody stood up straight with a huff. "We've got to

change it up before I deep lunge myself into something I'm not coming out of. My ass is killing me."

No kidding. Zack had spent too long in the shower this morning thinking about that very same topic.

"All right." Zack shook his head and waved back toward their cars. "Let's jog it back, and we'll do some arms on the steps before calling it." The sooner he got away and out of Brody's general vicinity, the better. There was only so much people watching he could do.

They fell into an easy rhythm, warmed up despite the early morning. Brody did his same power up at the end, this time attempting to cut Zack off. His competitiveness made Zack smile. Then he whipped Brody's ass effortlessly.

Brody was panting by the time they made it to the steps, bent over trying to catch his breath, and Zack grinned at his win while Brody glared.

"It's those damn legs of yours." Brody pulled at his tee and wiped at his mouth and forehead. "Moose legs." His shirt came up enough to show a long span of skin, the strength in his abs as he moved, and the cut of his hip, dusting of hair leading down into his shorts.

"You want some?"

Hell yes. "Huh?" Zack hoped his face didn't resemble a deer caught in headlights, center stage, in a packed stadium. "What?"

Brody gave him a bemused look and raised an eyebrow. He pointed over to his car. "I said I've got a couple of Gatorades. You want some?"

Zack nodded so he wouldn't have to speak and sound like an idiot. He slumped against the railing as Brody climbed the stairs. Then he remembered and called out, "Hey, we've got arms first!"

All he got in return was a dismissive snorting sound. It shouldn't make Zack smile, but it did. In fact, most of Brody made Zack smile. Whether he was as dry as protein powder or so damn determined and focused, in rare moments he laughed or smiled, or instead of being sexy as hell, he elevated their chitchat into some profound insight and knocked Zack on his ass—it was all attractive. Even moody and disgruntled, the man was still hot.

Normally Zack would be thinking, *He's gorgeous, sure, but*

straight. He would admire Brody and move on. But he didn't imagine what had happened the other day. The attraction wasn't completely one-sided. But Brody was either in denial or in the closet—*way* in—and Zack swore he'd never go there again. Everything in his logical side glowered at him, incredulous, yelling, *You, sir, are an idiot!*

But Brody made him want to go for it anyway. Leap in, both feet, in over his head. He might drown, but he'd think about it later. Incredulous logical guy was going to have a field day when this all ended with him drowning in his own stupidity.

Brody jogged back down, handing Zack a bright blue bottle before he sat down a few steps up. Dusting the sand off his hands before taking a long swallow from his drink, Zack decided it was time to carefully study the ingredients on the side of the bottle.

"So did I successfully distract you from the push-ups from hell?" Brody asked.

Zack looked up and laughed. Brody would never back out from training. Zack would bet his boat that after this drink he'd be bitching about getting his heart rate back up, but Zack played along. "I can let you off with a warning this time. Buuuut, we'll just double up next time."

Brody's mouth tugged up, just a little, his eyes crinkling in the corners. He took another swallow; this time his hand came to rest on his bad knee, thumb rubbing at the scar. Zack zeroed in on the movement, noticed the twitch of his foot.

"You all right?"

Brody nodded and took his hand away.

Zack wasn't convinced. "Sure you are." He took the couple of steps up to stand in front of Brody, hands going to his knee, supporting it as he stretched it out, bending the joint. Feeling the movement, the slide. He watched Brody's face to see if there was any expression of pain.

Brody stared back at him, hands pegged to his sides but his gaze firmly holding Zack's. There was absolutely no pain there. A shitload of other stuff but no pain. Intense and scrutinizing, it made Zack very aware that he stood between Brody's spread legs, hands on the warm, sandy skin of his knee and thigh. Hadn't they *just* been here?

That same heat and heaviness filled the air faster than smoke. It slowed everything down, sensitizing his fingertips to the fine hair covering firm muscles, the tensing of Brody's body, the smallest of contractions in his thigh. Zack set his leg down slowly, but left his hand just above the knee, his heart racing, thundering like he'd just sprinted the full length of Folly Beach. He was about to leap. It was insane, but he kept moving closer to the edge because there was no way he couldn't.

Brody didn't move. He sat there oozing power and destructive sex appeal like some statue of Ares come to life. Zack was having about a million internal explosions, and Brody's face was set like stone. Except for the desire so very apparent in his eyes. A need was there. No man looked at another man like that without it. Whether Brody realized it or not, it was burning from the inside, the stormy-gray gaze saying more than if Brody got up and yelled, *I want you! And I'm going to take you right here on this beach!*

Zack would let him too. He wanted Brody, and at the moment, he didn't care about logic or fallout or anything besides answering that look. Zack leaned forward and pressed his lips against Brody's.

They were firm and salty and sweet from the Gatorade. Brody didn't budge. He didn't move away or flinch, so Zack slid his lips over Brody's again, relishing the feel, the taste, the brush of Brody's stubble. He was about to pull away when he felt Brody's lips part. Pliant, softness giving way, allowing it to happen. The shock of want winded Zack. The slightest brush from the tip of his tongue, and he slid his hand around the back of Brody's neck, thinking of nothing but the pressure of Brody's lips against his and the shot of desire as he sucked Brody's bottom lip between his.

The front of his shirt wound tight before their lips were ripped apart. Brody slid back, looking debauched, thoroughly turned on, and *pissed as hell.*

Zack couldn't get the "Oops?" out of his mouth before he was shoved back a couple of steps.

Brody stood. He bristled before looking around. "What the fuck was that?"

Zack opened his mouth to state the obvious, but Brody

plowed on, eyes on fire with something far different than passion. "I'm not a fag," he ground out.

Zack took another step back. Brody was a lot of things, but he couldn't possibly be *that* much of an asshole. Zack was at a loss for words.

It only seemed to piss Brody off more, glaring hard enough to peel paint. "I said, I'm not gay."

"No. You said you're not a fag." Zack glared back, wishing he could rage at Brody with everything he had. "You sure about that?" he asked instead.

He pointed at Zack. "Fuck you." And with that, Brody was up the stairs and gone.

CHAPTER EIGHT

The knocking started again. What the hell? He could stand there all night and listen to Zack knocking, or he could answer the door. He knew it was Zack; he'd looked through the peephole. What was wrong with a six-foot-one, hundred-and-ninety-five pound, thirty-three-year-old policeman and homicide detective hiding behind a door from his physical therapist?

Everything. Brody needed his fucking head examined.

Fuck it.

"You're going to wear a hole in the damn door," he said as he jerked it open.

"Not if you'd answer it." Zack stood there, still looking beach swept even twenty-four hours later.

So Brody snapped, "What do you want?"

Zack looked at him like he'd asked what planet they were on. "What do you *think?* I want to talk to you about...you know." He tilted his head.

"Nothing to say." Brody moved to close the door on him.

Zack put his hand out to hold it open. "Five minutes, that's all I'm asking."

Brody wanted to, but he didn't close the door.

"I'm..." Zack paused. "I'm sorry. I was out of line yesterday, both professionally and personally." He lowered his voice. "I shouldn't have kissed you."

Brody's neighbor chose that moment to walk out the door with her bag of garbage. She probably hadn't heard a word, but she smiled at both of them like she knew exactly what was going on. Not that Zack would care. Brody, however, cared very much. He stepped back and waved Zack inside.

Zack complied and stepped just inside the door, closing it behind him.

Brody stood there, his back against one wall of the hall foyer, arms crossed over his chest.

"I shouldn't have kissed you," Zack repeated. "But it doesn't have to mean the end of us training together."

Brody didn't say a word, didn't move, and he could barely make eye contact. Zack kept talking.

"I misunderstood or misread...whatever. I don't know. But now I do know how you feel. It won't happen again. We'll just rewind to yesterday afternoon and...pretend nothing happened."

Brody's gaze darted down the hall to the kitchen and back again. Eventually he met Zack's gaze. "I can't pretend it didn't happen."

"Yes, you can." Zack's brown eyes were big and apologetic. "We go back to training. We run; we do what we've been doing for weeks. I made you a promise that I'd get you in shape. We have a business agreement, and I take my work very seriously."

"I know that."

"So let me finish helping you. It's just running and weights. We don't even have to talk. Not a word. Just work."

"You?" Brody cocked an eyebrow. "Not talk?" He found it hard to imagine. Zack not being able to talk could easily cause the big man to internally implode and form a black hole.

Never mind that he'd reluctantly miss all the chatter.

"I really am sorry, man," Zack said.

Brody could tell he meant it, but Zack being sorry wasn't the issue.

"I know." Brody again glanced the other way. Zack wasn't the only one who needed to own up to apologizing. "And I'm...I shouldn't have said what I said."

"That you're not a fag?"

Brody wanted to flinch, but he refused. "Yeah."

"I'll survive it. I'm gay, Brody. It's not the first time I've ever heard the word or had it flung at me."

Brody's eyes snapped back to Zack's. Imagine. To just be able to say it. To say it just like that. *I'm gay.* Like it was no big fucking deal. Like it wouldn't be the end of who you were. "You're a decent guy. I was out of line saying something like that to you."

"Okay, so, fair enough. We were both wrong, so we're even Steven. Tomorrow we can go right back to training like nothing ever happened."

"I..." Brody shook his head. "It's not that simple. I can't. It's too..." He pulled a face. "I can't jog with you every other day like it's nothing."

Zack nodded, the air around him changing to some defeated cloud that didn't suit the man at all. The broad shoulders sank; damn it but it made Brody want to say to hell with it. Anything to stop Zack looking like a kicked puppy.

"If I could forget it," Brody tried, "I would. But I can't. We can't be workout buddies. Trainer and trainee. Whatever. We can't meet up and pal around like I never kissed you. It doesn't work like that."

Zack blinked a few times and said nothing, and then he looked at Brody like they'd just met for the first time.

The confused look continued.

"What?" Brody asked.

"You mean like *I* never kissed *you*."

"That's what I said."

"*No.*" Zack shook his head. You said like *you* never kissed *me*. As in you"—he pointed to Brody—"kissing me"—then himself.

"No, I didn't." Brody knew his face was either going ghost white or fiery red. What the fuck?

"Yes. Yes, you did."

"Well, what the fuck ever. You know what I meant," Brody snapped.

"Brody, do you... If you need to talk to someone about this, we ca—"

"No! Do not start with me, Zack." Brody bowed up and

moved into Zack's personal space. The last thing he needed was to talk about any of this. Not with Zack, not with anyone. "I don't need to talk to *anyone*. Whatever fucking kind of mind tricks you think you're going to play, forget it."

"I'm not playing any mind tricks on you," Zack insisted. He didn't move. Didn't get into Brody's face but didn't back down either. "I think you're doing a good enough job mind fucking yourself."

"Fuck you!"

"You could if you weren't such an asshole, punishing yourself for being gay and living so damn deep in denial you can't even *see* straight much less *be* straight."

Brody shoved him back, pushed at his chest. "Get out. Get the fuck out of my house, right now."

Zack moved out of his path but didn't leave. "Shit. I didn't mean— You *have* to see what's going on here. You can't act like I'm making all this up. It isn't just me. I'm gay, not delusional."

Brody clenched his jaw, grinding his teeth, every muscle in his body tensing. Who the fuck did Zack think he was? Coming in here, acting like he knew jack shit about his life or anything else?

"Tell me why," Zack insisted. As always, he just wouldn't shut up. "Tell me why us kissing is the end of the goddamn world. You're not married. You're not even in a relationship…"

The man had no clue. No idea what it was like to live Brody's life, have his past, and live in his world. In Zack's life it didn't matter, it wasn't the end of his world, and it just made him all the more attractive. Shit. Brody wanted to live in that world, but Zack didn't.

"Brody." Zack moved back into his line of sight. "Talk to me. You're standing there like you want to beat the shit out of me, and I can tell you right now, I won't let that happen. Words. Use them. I'm not the damn enemy, I swear. Use your mouth, not your fist to—"

Brody grabbed him. He had no idea what he intended, but he felt trapped. Trapped in this hall, in life. Trapped in his fucking head, trapped by Zack, by everything. He had to get out. He gripped the front of his shirt and shoved Zack back against the wall, fully expecting him to come out swinging. Brody would if

someone did that to him. Instead Zack just looked at him. Ready
to defend himself but refusing to raise a hand against Brody.

And that was what sealed it. Part of him wanted to let loose
on Zack for being everything he'd denied for so long. He'd fought
against it, lied about it, snuck around, and hid like the fucking
coward he really was. He could blame Zack, and they'd go down
swinging, probably beating the shit out of each other until he was
too bloody and battered to hate anymore.

But Zack just stood there. Big brown eyes still as sincere,
still as accepting. Handsome face wanting to understand what
Brody couldn't express. Wanting to help. Wanting to know.
Wanting...Brody.

He pushed Zack again. One last aggressive opposition, one
last time, one last failed effort at denial. This time, Brody followed
the movement because there was nothing else for him to do. He
kissed Zack like he was the only way to survive.

Zack fell back against the wall and took Brody with him. He
let himself be taken. He clung to Zack, lips hard on his. Desperate.
Demanding. Zack opened, letting Brody in before taking more.
Sucking and thrusting his tongue against Brody's, he ran his
hands down Brody's back to his waist and drew him closer. Warm,
sure hands on his lower back, the contact made Brody catch his
breath.

Friction. The possibility for such delicious friction.

Zack dragged his hands up Brody's arms, over his
shoulders, and into his hair. He tugged gently and leaned back to
look deep into Brody's eyes.

Zack didn't speak, but his eyes said it all. They promised
this was okay and that Zack wanted this just as much and for just
as long. And he wasn't going to say a word about it.

This time, Brody let Zack kiss him. He opened for Zack and
the delicious slide of their tongues, the sucking tug at his bottom
lip.

God, he'd imagined this. Dreamed about it and then wanted
to beat himself up for it. But how could this be wrong? Everything
about it felt so right.

Brody relaxed his hands and spread his fingers against
Zack's chest. The heat scorching through the T-shirt, the hard

muscle of Zack's pecs, the rapid-fire of the heart within his chest. He needed skin. Brody had to see and touch all that tan skin. Feel it against his. He wanted his body melded to Zack's until he couldn't fucking breathe for the closeness.

"I got it," Zack said, and Brody realized he'd been pulling desperately at Zack's T-shirt. "Yours too." Zack tugged at the bottom of Brody's shirt, and they both parted quickly to shed them and rejoin.

"God. You feel even better than you look," Zack said, breathing into his ear, pressing himself in so Brody could feel him everywhere.

Zack felt like sin worth dying for, but Brody couldn't get out the words. All he knew was the room was spinning, and he never wanted it to stop. He rubbed up Zack's arms, his back. Zack's erection dug into his hip, and he wanted to see it. See it. Touch it. Taste it.

Zack's mind must've gone in the same direction, because it was only seconds before his hands were pushing at the small of Brody's back, pressing him in, tilting his hips so that Zack's erection wasn't the only one making itself known. He slid his hands lower, dipping them inside the back of Brody's basketball shorts. Lower still, his fingers skimming the top of his ass.

It should've brought Brody back to reality, shaken him out of this delicious mistake. It only dragged him in further.

Zack's hands on him. Big. Strong. So sure and certain of what he wanted. He touched Brody without the hesitation of doubt or shame. Brody dropped his head into the crook of Zack's shoulder, the scent of him overwhelming. Brody licked and nipped at the sensitive skin there. There was a rumble in Zack's chest, so Brody kissed him and started all over again.

Zack cupped Brody's ass with both hands, massaging, kneading the muscle, worshipping it and making the shorts fall lower.

"This okay?" he asked and breathed a short laugh. "I can't believe I'm even asking. Please say it's okay."

Brody could only nod and step into him, one foot between Zack's, one thigh between his.

"Your ass is amazing. Looks it. Now I know, feels it too."

Zack slid Brody's shorts farther down until his hard cock bounced up between them. "So is this." Zack's hand was on him immediately.

Brody had never been touched with so much confidence, handled with such assurance. Zack stroked him and made a low sound of approval.

"My *God*. Should've known you'd be hung like a damn stallion."

Brody smiled against Zack's neck before he could catch it.

"I know that got a smile. Don't bother fighting it," Zack said. The pleasure in his voice made Brody's chest ache. The fact that this was okay, that touching and wanting was okay. Zack could smile and laugh like it was all so natural, and he could make Brody do the same.

He stroked Brody again, all the way up and down. Up and down, then cupping his balls, rolling them in his hand until Brody's eyes rolled back in his head.

"I've wanted this. Even when I knew it was unprofessional, could get me fired, I wanted this." Zack stroked him again as he rocked his own erection against Brody's thigh. He rocked again and again before taking Brody's hand in a loose hold and placing it over where he strained against his shorts.

Brody cupped him, feeling the moisture through the clothing. Pressure first and slow rubs through the cotton. Brody had done this before, but this was different. This was someone he knew. Liked. Wanted to see again.

Zack's breathing caught, then a long exhale. He was into Brody's touch just as much, and that knowledge made Brody bolder. Made him want skin, the heat of Zack, to feel *him*. He worked the button and zipper of Zack's shorts, Zack wriggling to help but never letting go or slowing his strokes. Once he worked Zack's boxers down just low enough, he reached inside and touched him. The long, hot length of Zack like living fire in his hand. Brody rubbed his thumb over the tip, gathering the moisture before taking Zack in his fist.

Zack's head fell back, the arch of the neck so vulnerable yet strong that Brody had to kiss him there again.

He kissed and stroked, his rhythm imperfect because Zack's

touch was driving him out of his mind.

"Yeah." Zack moaned, his voice low and rolling over every inch of Brody's bare skin. "Perfect. Oh..."—a guttural roll of sound—"so damn perfect."

He took Brody's mouth again. Harsh. Demanding but somehow still giving. Brody gave back, their strokes faster, tighter. Bucking against each other, barreling toward what lay ahead. They both wanted this too much, had waited too long.

He dug his free hand into Zack's arm, imagining if this was what it felt like to get off on Zack, he couldn't imagine fucking.

"Oh...*fuck*, yeah." Brody heard himself groan when Zack moved his grip and focused on the head of his cock.

Fuck yeah was right. He was going to come. He was going to come with Zack's hands all over him and his tongue in his mouth, and he could think of no better way on Earth. He stroked Zack harder, tighter, feeling his entire body buck against him.

"Yeah...me too. Oh yeah, *God*, me too." Zack let his head roll forward before it fell back again, the strain of his orgasm showing in the thick vein along his neck, the tension of his shoulders. The climax had him tightening his fist around Brody's cock, and it shoved Brody over the edge.

Zack's slick warmth spilled over his hand as Brody came too. Hard and fast and never ending. He bit into Zack's bottom lip as they sank to the floor.

CHAPTER NINE

Z ack stared at the ceiling. Beside him, Brody still breathed heavy and deep. He could see the broad chest rising and falling in his peripheral vision. That gorgeous chest, muscled and sprinkled with dark hair. He could easily imagine lying on that chest. Leaning over, into it as he pushed his way inside Brody. Imagined it warm and full against his back too, as Brody pushed his way into him.

All of it sounded divine. Sign him up yesterday.

That was, unless Brody did another one-eighty on him in mere seconds. One moment blissed out on sex, the next raging against his own homosexuality and the world; he put none of it past the unpredictable detective.

Zack risked a glance over. Brody sat bare-assed on the foyer rug, his eyes hooded and looking sexier than hell. Zack grabbed his T-shirt off the floor, cleaned them both up, then wadded it into a ball. Neither of them said a word as they pulled up and adjusted their shorts and sat there on the floor.

Brody leaned back against the wall, drawing his knees up to rest his elbows on them and run his hands through his hair. He stayed that way, head resting in his hands. Silent.

Please, hell no. Not the denial. Not the self-recrimination, the claims this never happened. The anger, loathing, and self-destruction. The fury at Zack because he'd brought out the truth. He couldn't take any more of the BS, and he'd end up trying to shake sense into Brody. Shaking a man Brody's size would not be easy either.

Brody turned his head, keen gray eyes a deeper shade—

sharper. Zack found himself holding his breath as he listened.

"I knew I should've stayed in therapy with that dipshit Matt," Brody said, the slightest curve to his lips. "You've been nothing but fucking trouble."

Zack felt a tension in his chest release. He allowed himself to breathe. And hope. "I never claimed otherwise."

The curve grew into a half smile before Brody's face pulled tight. "No one knows," he said.

"I figured as much." Zack felt his stomach fall as he waited for the worst to come.

"Not at work. Not anyone around here. Except for you, obviously."

Obviously. "But...you've done this before." Zack nodded.

"Yeah. Enough to get by. But never here and never with someone I already knew in day-to-day life." Brody looked around. "That makes me sound pathetic, I know." He let out a dry laugh as he let his head fall back. "I can't believe we just did that in my hallway."

He didn't sound upset, but with Brody, it was hard to tell.

"You've never been with someone..." Zack wasn't even sure how to finish the question. "In your home?"

"No," Brody said. He shrugged. "If I'm out of town, I go out. Sometimes I go out of town just so I can go out."

It wasn't the time to dive into all that Q and A, although Zack knew eventually they'd have to. There was so much to talk about it if they were going to be more than one handjob in the hall. But for now, it was enough that Brody was talking and was not freaking the fuck out. That was all he could hope for and more than he expected.

"I know how to be discreet," Zack said without Brody asking.

Brody's gaze shot to his, some kind of promise making his eyes flash. Zack shouldn't have offered, but the look of, what? Being finally understood? It tugged at Zack's heart. This was stupid; Zack was being stupid. He wasn't in the closet, and he had no desire to live in someone else's. But if he had to play it cool to be with Brody, he would. For now. And hope to God it didn't blow up on him like it had before.

Shit. Napalm was more like it. Full-scale bombing of his life. What the hell was he thinking even trying this?

"Guess this means we're still running tomorrow?" Brody asked.

Zack nodded.

"The things you'll do just to get a man to jog." His face was so expressionless, voice so dry that Zack had to laugh.

"You got me." Zack smiled and pushed himself up. He held a hand out to help Brody up.

Brody rose, and his eyes lingered on every inch of Zack as he got up. Zack was sure he swelled a few inches in height, in other places too, at that look. Brody. All that power, most of which he hadn't yet seen at fully healed capacity, the sharp mind, the acidic humor... How was Zack supposed to turn away from that? Say no to looks like that from a man like Brody?

Say to himself: *Self, he's simply too much trouble. He's clearly got issues and some major baggage. And he's so deep in the closet he can barely be out to himself. Run, don't walk, away from him. Never mind that he's unlike anyone you've ever met. Smart, sharp as a scalpel, challenges you, built like a brick house, makes you laugh, and keeps you on your toes. Never a dull moment. And let's be honest, the cop thing is a huge turn-on. But forget all that and move on because it's not going to be easy.*

How could he do that?

One simple answer: he couldn't.

Brody stepped into him, a hand barely touching Zack's arm, before pulling him in by the elbow. "I won't lie. This freaks me out, but... I'm glad you showed up and beat my door down, not shutting up until you made your point," he said.

"You're so freaking weird." Zack cracked up, his laugh filling the hallway. "And I like it." Then he kissed Brody. Long and lingering and sure to give them both something to think about until they met again.

—*—

The next day they met on the beach, this time only running, but covering the length of Folly Beach coastline—from the washout where surfers laid claim to the State Park, where there wasn't a soul at this hour. They ran the whole distance, alternately talking about the beach and Zack's surfing or in a companionable silence in which all Zack could do was think about riding the waves versus riding Brody.

"Should've known you'd love to surf," Brody said as they neared the beach access close to Zack's house.

"What's that supposed to mean?" He had to work not to snicker with glee at the images in his dirty mind.

"You've got the floppy hair and the tan. And that laid-back way surfers carry themselves. Except in the PT room. In there, you're a hard-ass."

"Thanks. I'll take that as a compliment."

"It's meant as one. You're not laid-back about your job, no bullshit about work."

"Oh, I thought you were complimenting my actual ass. Darn," he teased.

Brody shoved him as they ran. "I'm being serious. You're dedicated to your job. That's how it should be."

Zack ran ahead a little and turned to salute him as they neared the steps.

"Smart-ass."

"Ah, come on. You did sound a *little* like a police chief there. I had to."

Something passed in Brody's eyes. Darkness more than the stormy gray. He was suddenly stern and hardened. Angry, but not with Zack. It was probably twisted how much that look turned him on.

Brody cracking dry jokes and smirking was undeniably hot. Brody dark and dangerous did crazy, strange things to his insides. It made him want to jump into that deadly, churning water just to know the rush it'd provide. Angry sex with Brody would no doubt be the best sex of his life. Of this he was certain.

They slowed to a jog, and the darkness finally lifted as Brody punched Zack in the arm with a smirk. "How about next time I won't say shit to compliment you? You suck. How's that?"

He couldn't help it. He cracked up and had to start walking. "Well...as a matter of fact. Yes I do. And I'm excellent at that too."

Brody started walking as well, his gaze narrowed, trying hard to look disapproving as he shook his head. The hint of a grin gave him away. "You have no shame." It didn't sound like he minded either.

That was it. They needed to get naked ASAP. Why the hell not? They'd laid a few ground rules. What they did, they kept private, and Zack was clearly the more experienced. How much more? It didn't matter. All he cared about was Brody all sweaty and salty, his dark hair sticking up in places. Brody would frown about it if he knew, because it made him look less threatening. His T-shirt clung to him in deliciously naughty ways and, from the not so secretive glances he kept throwing at Zack's chest, Zack could only imagine his shirt was doing the same.

"No shame whatsoever." Screw it. Zack threw caution to the wind and just came out with it.

"My house is just up there." He thumbed to the road beyond the beach access. "I'm one street back. Come on, I have water and Gatorade and the walk will help cool the muscles." He turned and started walking, leaving Brody—and any chance to protest—a few steps behind.

"Water sounds good," Brody said, catching up to walk beside him.

He bit back a smile. Operation Get Brody in the House *and* Naked, so far a success.

"This is your place?" Brody asked as they reached the driveway.

"Nah, it's someone else's. I'm hoping they won't notice the two big, sweaty men in their kitchen, drinking up all their water."

That earned him a shove to the back of the head. It shouldn't have been sexually charged, but with Brody, it seemed 90 percent of everything crackled with carnal tension.

He unlocked the door with the key from the little pocket of his shorts and let Brody into the well-air-conditioned abode of Shack de Zack.

Brody's grin snuck out upon entry. "This is absolutely your place." He went straight to the enormous painted African mask on the wall between the kitchen and living room. The one that hung between his two palm plants, above his collection of snow globes from all his travels.

"Pretty much." Zack opened the fridge and grabbed two waters.

"It's random as hell." Brody chuckled. "Fess up, you own a beanbag chair, don't you?"

"Maybe."

"And I bet you blast Bob Marley on the weekends while you drink a beer with some kind of fruit in it, sitting outside and watching the sun go down, contemplating the awesomeness of life." Brody took the offered water.

"I hear the sarcasm, but as a matter of fact, hell yeah. Marley is awesome for unwinding, and nothing beats a Corona on a summer night." He took a sip of his water and smiled, noting that Brody was openly joking with him. He wasn't about to point it out, but the hard-ass cop had a playful side.

Brody shook his head again, cracking his beer open. "You were probably just the kind of kid I got calls on when I was a uni. College kids either drinking beer or smoking pot in the park, not a care in the world, not a clue either. Solving the world's problems when they have none."

"Hey, I'm only five years younger than you."

"Yeah, and I was in the uniform at twenty-two."

"Oh."

"Yeah, oh." Brody gave him a knowing look.

That dark-eyed warning he probably used all the time at work. He was every bit the uniformed officer who would've told teenage Zack and his premed friends to put the beer in the garbage can and get their asses out of the park and back to campus before they got themselves a record.

"I hauled in a few guys just like you back in the day. Harmless, but scared them enough to stay out of trouble in the future."

Damn. All Zack could think was the man needed to be pounced. And *soon*. He eyed Brody tilting back the bottled water like he'd done a three-day desert trek. Now he didn't have to hide it when he watched the way Brody's throat moved. No longer had to disguise checking him out. It sure as hell made their run a lot more motivating. Slowing down occasionally to run behind Brody was an experience not to be missed. They ought to put the man at the front of marathons. Straight women and gay men would all cut their times in half.

A wayward bead of sweat ran down Brody's strong neck into his T-shirt. Stupid fucking T-shirt hid way too much of the good stuff. It had to go.

Zack laughed because maybe now he could say exactly that and not get decked. He wouldn't risk being that überbossy just yet, though.

"What are you laughing about now?" Brody asked, his tone brusque but playful. "You think I'm fucking weird? *You* are weird. Laughing at nothing. Tapestry-hanging, candle-lighting, and incense-loving beach boy. What the fuck have I gotten myself into?"

Zack snorted with laughter as he put his water down and closed in on Brody. Gray eyes homed in on him over the top of the bottle. He reached out and pulled the bottle away from Brody's lips.

"Nuh-uh." Brody grinned. "This one is mine. Get your own damn water."

"I don't want your drink, dickhead." He laughed again.

"No?"

"No." He took the drink from Brody and set it aside. He stepped in closer, one hand on the counter behind him, the other hovering at Brody's side. He waited, wanting to know what Brody would do or say, if anything.

Brody's heated gaze alternated between Zack's mouth and eyes. His lips went from curled in amusement to barely parted as he waited too. "You really are a fucking tease," he finally said.

"Kinda." Zack grinned before closing the last inches to take Brody's mouth with his.

This time he wanted to take his time. Savor the taste of Brody in a way he couldn't when it was frantic and desperate. The cool feel of his tongue, sucking on it suggestively enough for Brody to grab his hips and tug him in.

He had other ideas. He pulled back and reached for Brody's water, the movement causing his erection to brush against Brody's hip. He took a long swallow, eyeing Brody's face.

"What are you doing?"

Zack smiled. "Thirsty," he said, just before Brody shook his head and jerked the bottle away, turning them to press Zack back against the counter. Brody palmed the back of Zack's head and pulled him down, angling his head to deepen the kiss. Brody's tongue slid against his as he curled his fingers into Zack's hair and tugged.

That bolt of want thrummed through his body at the taste of Brody. The brush of his stubble burning his mouth, one hand pushing against his chest, holding him there, fingers clenched in his, the other holding his head still.

Zack found the loose band of Brody's shorts and brushed his fingers along the seam. There was a muffled sound of approval before Brody sucked at his tongue and spread his fingers wide against his shirt.

"Stupid shirts," Zack mumbled.

"What?" Brody said on a huff of a laugh.

He moved just enough to be able to tug at Brody's shirt, jerking it up because it now offended him in *every* way.

Brody let him yank it up over his head. "What'd my shirt ever do to you?" he asked.

Zack tossed it on the floor behind him. "I couldn't stop staring at you while we ran. Thinking."

Brody shook his head, a hint of a smile. "What's that got to do with my poor shirt?"

He grabbed Brody by the waist, locking their hips together so there was no way Brody could miss the hard-on and he couldn't miss Brody's either. "It's got to do with me wanting you naked."

Brody leaned in, kissing him, but he wriggled out of his shorts and toed off his shoes and socks, lips not leaving Zack's until he spoke. "Happy now?"

Zack looked down, slow gaze up, taking in all of Brody. Brody, once someone he figured he'd never see again, standing before him like this. "Oh yeah." Brody totally naked, in his kitchen, his hard dick catching on Zack's shorts, his broad chest warming Zack through his clothes...

He groaned and clutched Brody's ass, pressing their cocks together, rubbing as Brody made a low growling noise. Zack controlled the slow grind with his hands, turning them again, the hot pleasure curling in his stomach and deep into his balls.

The pressure was bliss but not enough for either of them to get off. He was nothing if not resourceful. He left Brody's mouth to suck down his jaw, the late-day shadow rough on his tongue. He paused long enough to suck hard at the cord of muscle in Brody's shoulder, and then Brody was tugging at his shirt too.

He looked at Brody, mouth swollen and eyes dark.

"I'm pissed at your shirt too."

Zack grinned but kept working his way down. "I'm busy," he said before sucking at the definition of Brody's pec, flicking his tongue over a dark nipple, the taut stomach, taking particular care to lick near the dent of his hips.

Brody groaned and faltered on his feet. A quick intake of breath when Zack brushed his cheek past Brody's erection. Bobbing, pink and hard—like he could miss it? Of course Brody would have a gorgeous cock. It shouldn't surprise him. He even smelled amazing. Clean sweat, cologne, and man. His cock twitched against Zack's cheek, and an honest-to-God moan came out of the man.

Zack looked up to find Brody entranced. Staring down, eyes blazing, jaw tense and set to crack.

"Zack," he said. "You start teasing me now, and I'll kick your ass."

He wasn't that cruel. Never mind he wanted his mouth on that cock like fifteen minutes ago.

He gave the head a few little licks before leaning in and sliding it between his lips. Brody instantly wound up like a spring, and Zack squeezed his ass, drawing him into his mouth, slowly and fully.

He felt Brody's weight shift as he grabbed the counter.

"Fuck." Brody groaned.

Exactly.

Zack slid him in and out, just enough suction to get him going but not enough to finish him off. He wasn't interested in a race. He settled his knees on the pile of Brody's clothing, caressing Brody's thighs and back up to cup his ass. A quick sucking pop on the head, and he was rewarded with a jerk of Brody's hips. Zack licked his way down the shaft and flicked his tongue over Brody's balls.

A touch against the back of his head, Brody's fingers in his hair. Zack glanced up, and Brody's gaze was still as hot, just as focused.

"Zack," he tried, his voice raspy and full of need.

Zack kept his eyes locked on Brody's and took him back into his mouth, sucking hard, deep enough to touch the back of his throat before working him in and out, hot and fast.

Brody groaned again, face stained a luscious pink. "Fuck...Zack. Yeah."

He would've grinned with pride if he weren't busy with more important things. He already knew eye contact did things to Brody, and he went with it. Relished it too. He wanted to make Brody come. Not just come hard, but the kind of neck-arching, back-locking, hard climax that made you feel like your spine might crack. This orgasm would be carved into Brody's mind. The kind he'd think about weeks, even years later.

Brody watched him, eyes glassy. He licked and bit at his bottom lip, still stroking Zack's hair with a shaky hand, probably trying not to dig his fingers in and hold Zack in place so he could fuck his mouth.

Not that Zack would mind, but they could do that some other time. When it came to that, he'd let Brody control the rhythm, everything. Right now, Zack wanted things his way, and his way meant Brody bellowing out his climax.

He paused long enough to lick at his fingers before taking Brody back in. Using his wet fingers to slide behind Brody's sack and press, making light circles, he added pressure. Pressure and what he knew was undeniable pleasure. With his longest finger, he brushed back, barely touching the opening. Just a taunt of what could be.

Brody groaned, and finally, his hips did move. He thrust,

and Zack only had to suck a few seconds more, massaging Brody harder, with all he had, teasing him with promises of more.

"Fuck! *Fuuuuuck*," he shouted, bent over, one hand tightening in Zack's hair, the other digging into his shoulder.

Warm bursts of salty flavor as he swallowed down. Zack was so painfully hard in his shorts that the slightest touch, and he'd be coming too.

"Zack." Brody leaned against him, his face flushed and relaxed, mouth parted, eyes closed. "I think you killed me."

Not hardly, but that feeling was definitely Zack's aim. He rocked back on his heels and looked up at Brody.

Chin rested against his chest, arms dangling loosely by his sides like the bones were gone, Brody sighed heavy and deep. He eventually lifted his chin and met Zack's gaze. Hooded eyes, finally warm and clear. A smirk curled the edge of his lips.

"C'mere." Brody tugged Zack up to his feet and turned him so his back was to the cabinet. His kiss was languid. Relaxed. He took his time exploring, sucking at Zack's bottom lip, big hands curling into his waist until it brought a moan from both of them.

Brody eased his way down to one knee, the movement awkward because of the injury.

"Oh hell no." Zack grabbed his arm and urged him back up. "We are not going to undo all the good we've done, no matter how damn eager I am. Come on." He led Brody into his living room and over to the huge chair. Shoving the ottoman out of the way, he indicated for Brody to sit.

"Damn, you're bossy."

"No, I'm smart." He grinned.

"And so humble." Brody tugged him in and kissed him again, slid his tongue against Zack's, sucking and nibbling his bottom lip until he was set to explode.

"I'm a tease?"

"Shirt." Brody snapped his fingers. "Your turn now. Off."

He yanked his shirt up over his head, smiling as he felt Brody tugging his shorts down. He stepped out of his shoes and socks and stood naked before the sexiest lover he'd ever had. Not mere physicality, but the essence of Brody. The kind of man spelled capital *M-A-N*. And as Brody sat down on the chair and pulled Zack forward with his hands on the backs of his thighs, he realized he was going to last about five seconds with this *M-A-N* sucking his cock.

Brody glanced up at him, his eyes reflecting the slightest vulnerability, like when he'd faltered on his crutches. The human side to the guarded cop only made him more desirable, and, as he took Zack into his mouth, Zack realized he'd probably done this only a handful of times. Brody was definitely the type more likely to receive head than give it if he was cruising. It wasn't like he would've had to try hard either. Cruising some dance club, a man like Brody wouldn't have to work at finding an eager volunteer. The guys would've fallen all over themselves to suck him off.

Zack sympathized with them.

Brody's eyes fluttered closed, and he moaned as he sucked Zack in farther. Dark lashes against his olive skin. When he glanced back up, he nailed Zack with a look so deep, so intense, Zack felt *his* knees falter.

Enthusiasm and a driven purpose took the place of finesse and technique. He hadn't the experience of Zack, but it was just as well. That piled on top of Brody's fingers gripping the meat of his leg, urging him, wanting him, would've made Zack blow a fuse in the first three seconds. His gaze was at once glassy with pleasure and demanding in intent.

Zack had to lean forward and grab hold of Brody's shoulder; his orgasm was already coming on so strong. The tips of his fingers brushed against something raised and smooth. A quick glance told him a scar of some kind. He hadn't noticed it before. As he tried to look, Brody distracted him, his hand wrapped around Zack's cock, now working him too.

"Shit, Brody," he muttered.

Brody kept his gaze on Zack's face, letting go and urging him in so deep he hit the back of Brody's throat.

"Yeah. Shit, yeah..." Zack dug his fingers into the firm shoulder and came so hard he saw sparks. Brody never moved except to hold him tight as he rode wave after wave of his orgasm.

"Fuh-ucking hell." Zack stumbled back after, sitting down hard on his bare ass.

Brody looked at him from his seat on the chair, holding his body so tight one might think his limbs were about to shoot off in four different directions.

Zack flopped back, rolling his head to the side to look over at him. "Go on without me!" He waved with intentional dramatic flair. "Save yourself. Leave me here. I'm useless to anyone now."

Brody chuckled a bit, relaxing the slightest.

Good. That was the point.

"So that was..." Brody waited, shifted his weight, eyebrows cocked up.

Zack eased up to one elbow, body feeling twice its weight. "Was...?" He gave Brody a matching look.

"Okay?"

Zack sat straight up. "Okay? *Okay?* Dude! Are you asking or saying, because that was a helluva lot better than okay."

Brody dropped his head, and Zack worried until he heard the laughter and saw his shoulders moving with a low chuckle. It warmed Zack to his toes.

"I was asking. Relax. Your shameless pride in your skill is warranted. It's just...I don't... I haven't—"

"I know." Zack scooted closer and pushed himself up to his knees in front of Brody. "You're not one to bestow that gift on many. I get it." He leaned forward and slid his hand around to the back of Brody's head, tugging him forward. "And again I say that was a helluva lot better than okay."

He kissed him, at first soft and gentle. It took about ten seconds for it to grow heated enough that Brody's hands were on his arms, hauling him up and in.

Zack eased back. "If we start this again, you're going to have to carry me from this chair because my legs will cease to function. And I don't look it, but I'm heavy as hell."

"You look it."

"Hey!"

Brody smirked. "But I'd manage."

He just bet Brody would. There was a lot more to the man than anyone would first guess, and hadn't he always known? It was part of what drew Zack in. The complexity, the mystery, the hidden depths.

But damn, he didn't need to lose himself in the pleasure of digging. It was one thing to admire Brody, lust after him and not hide it anymore, and get to sate that desire. That was it, though. There would be no give and take between them other than the physical. And Zack needed to remind himself of that. Repeatedly.

There'd be no, *So let me introduce you to my friends. Take you to a hospital event. Meet my mom. Meet your fam!*

He was Brody's dirty little secret, and he better not forget it. He wouldn't, because he remembered exactly how it had felt with Marcus. When the only man he'd ever loved, the only one he'd gone so far as to entertain the cohabitation, long-time, maybe-forever notion with, ripped out his heart with two short sentences—it'd stunned him. Then he stomped on Zack's heart by marrying his old sweetheart from high school. All of it was like being blindsided by a Mack truck.

"Hey." Brody nudged him. "Did you already pass out on me?"

Zack tried shaking off the ghosts of the past.

"I'm getting engaged to Reena. Forget you ever knew me, because I have to forget you."

Marcus was gone, and it'd taken years to recover.

"Postcoital narcolepsy. Just tired," Zack lied. He was smarter now, and he wasn't doing that again. Not with Brody. Not with anyone, ever. He'd enjoy this time, but he'd remember what it was. A secret fling. Fun and light.

Temporary.

CHAPTER TEN

Brody's desk chair squeaked in protest as he leaned back as far as it would allow. The air-conditioning rattled the wall vent with its piss-poor effort to cool the room, and the wave of stifling heat that blasted the doorway with every entry and exit confirmed it was just another oppressively hot and humid day in Charleston.

Yet he'd give his left kidney to be trudging out in the heat instead of stuck in the damn office with his knee in its strap. Light duty was obviously code for the circle of hell designed especially for him.

He was back on the job now, so he should be happy with that. And at least his paperwork would be fucking perfect and he had access to his real case.

He stared at the white sea of his computer screen, seeing nothing. Instead he went over the Strangler case in his mind, hoping that something would magically pop up that he hadn't already considered.

It was a decent enough distraction from the fact that he was still treated as an invalid, stuck behind a desk. It also stopped him thinking about Zack. Kind of.

Thinking about Zack within these walls was uncomfortable to say the least. Confusing, new, disturbing. It gave him a headache from the tug-of-war going on upstairs. Downstairs, there was absolutely no conflict. None. Zack was all kinds of his type and he wouldn't bother denying it, but his mind couldn't meld the man Brody enjoyed spending time with and getting naked with, to the Brody of Charleston's Homicide Division.

Hell.

He wished he could shut down one part of himself, one way or the other. Either accept that he was into men and decide he didn't care what that meant to anyone, including himself, his deceased father, or his closest friends. *Or* give it all up, forget men and that aspect of life, and live only for the job.

If anyone could do it, he could. Police work was essentially a bubble he'd lived in his entire life. Granddad was a cop. Dad was a cop. He joined the force liked his dad, worked his ass off as a uni, and quickly moved into Homicide. Being the son of the ex-captain, it was what was expected of him, and he always did exactly what was expected.

He almost had the ideal life. Except for the fact that his life ended when his shift did. He had no life outside the job—until now. Work alone was no longer enough.

"What's up, Brody?" A detective from Vice passed his desk. "Good to see you back, man. Real good." He shook Brody's hand, and, with manly slaps on the back, the welcome was over.

Would he be so welcoming if he knew about last night? If he knew how much Brody enjoyed having Zack's dick in his mouth. Having his down Zack's throat.

It wasn't anyone's business, but if Brody came out, his private life would suddenly become everybody's business. It'd be the biggest thing to hit the department, and he could kiss the camaraderie and any future here good-bye. He'd seen it happen before.

His dad had been everything and all Brody strived to be. Well-respected, stand-up guy, hardworking cop. Brody had worked his ass off to live up to his dad's standards.

His expectations.

But he'd *expected* Brody to work his ass off. Expected him to be the best, to be proud of him. Brody remembered the way he'd looked at his retirement party. Dark eyes crinkled with fondness, blinking back the mist of saying good-bye to what had been a lifetime. His big forearms tightened as he held Brody. *"I'm proud of you, son. I can go, knowing you're here. A Brody will always be here for our city."*

To think, his dad never knew what a bullshit facade it all

really was.

Brody knew *what* he was, and he was *not* a man in his father's book. Real men did not fuck other men. A lesson he'd learned a long time ago.

"*He better hope he stays clean,*" one of the officers commented about a cop transferring out of the city. A cop whose personal life wasn't so secret.

"*I don't know,*" another one said. "*If he likes taking it up the ass, prison might be the best place for him.*"

His dad had laughed just as hard as the rest of them. Choice comments spilled out about men who were into other men. It wasn't the first he'd heard it either. Sideways remarks about homos and faggots were in his home his entire life. Enough so that any feeling he had besides hard work, things his dad could be *proud* of, were shoved far, far away.

But that day, his dad's laughter in the group was the only thing Brody had heard. He'd never been anything but a lie to his father, because the truth would've broken them.

There was no other way.

"Daaaamn, brother. Paperwork ain't that fucking bad." Lamont's deep, taunting voice rose over the computer monitor.

Brody shook off the creeping strangulation of the past and looked up at his massive partner. "It *is* that fucking bad," he said. "It's always that fucking bad."

"Ah!" Lamont waved him off and plopped what had to be a two-ton brown grocery sack on his desk. "That's because you can't type and it takes you all damn day, sitting there, huntin' and peckin'. Now move this shit out of the way." He nodded to the files and papers all over the end of Brody's desk.

"What's in the bag?" It hit the metal desk sounding heavy enough to contain a DB, but smelled like heaven...so he was going to guess it was Felicia's home cooking. He leaned in to take a bigger whiff.

"Man, get back." Lamont shoved him and moved the rest of the binders out of the way. "Felicia felt sorry for you not being out with me, and she said I should feed you so you'll get better. You're welcome."

Brody didn't wait for any other prompting. He dove right into the grocery bag and began hauling out Tupperware containers. Felicia's cooking was legendary.

Lamont jerked the bag away halfway through. "You need to fucking chill and let me get a plate before you start gnawing chicken with nothing but your bare hands. Hang on." He went in search of plates from the break room, and Brody did exactly as Lamont predicted.

He grabbed a breast of fried chicken that sat on top of the rest and sank his teeth into it without so much as a napkin nearby. Crispy outside, bursting with tender juicy goodness inside. He could star in the commercial if Felicia ever caved and finally opened a restaurant.

"Holy shit, that's good," he mumbled over a mouthful.

"Barn," Lamont scoffed as he pulled the chair around from his desk and set up two plates. "You were raised in a damn barn. Pass the chicken." He proceeded to load his plate with something from all of Felicia's delicacies until it looked like a damn photo spread from *Southern Living*.

Brody was licking his fingers from finishing the chicken before he ever even got to the plate business. Black-eyed peas, greens, macaroni and cheese, and corn bread. He was going to be in a food coma by the time lunch was over.

"I love your wife," Brody mumbled over his mac and cheese.

"As you should. But you can't have her." Lamont ate his black-eyed peas with the grace of an English aristocrat.

Brody already had a grease stain on his tie.

"What smells so good?" Griggs, another homicide detective, asked as he passed by.

"None-ya," Lamont barked.

Griggs flipped them both the bird and kept walking.

"If that motherfucker says one more thing about black people liking fried chicken, I'm whipping his ass and blaming you." Lamont wiped at his mouth. "I can't believe I gotta be his partner till you get back. Please hurry the fuck up, or *I* will commit homicide."

Brody laughed so hard he almost choked on a pea. "Damn,

I've missed you. And it's not about black people," he said, reaching for more chicken. "It's Southerners. Griggs is from Ohio. He doesn't know shit. You should ignore him, but if you kick his ass, I have your back. Is that...?" Brody leaned up out of his chair, spying one last pink container left in the bag.

Lamont was already jerking the bag away.

"Is that dessert?" Brody grabbed for it. "Don't even play. Is that peach cobbler?"

"Maybe."

He sat down with a happy sigh. It was absolutely peach cobbler, and he wasn't going to be able to move in about ten more minutes. "I needed this," Brody confessed. He was fully aware that with Lamont, *almost* every wall came down. He could be himself a bit.

Breathe.

"Why, are you that hungry?" Lamont poured himself some more tea.

"No, jackass. This." He pointed back and forth between them. "And this." He pointed to the room. "Even fucking Griggs. I was gone too long. It messes with your mind. Vacation is one thing, but..." He shook his head and had another bite.

"I know. More than a week, and you start twitching like a junkie. When I was out with the baby...damn. Felicia was begging me to go back to work. All, *I love you baby, but you're getting on my damn nerves. Bye!*"

Their mutual laughter filled the office at his impersonation of his wife. He could sound just like her.

"When are you back on active?" Lamont asked.

"Sooner the better. I don't do any testing for a few more weeks. Until then, this is my job."

"You'll end up with a gut if we eat like this all the time and you riding a desk."

"Nah." He wouldn't. Not if he or Zack had anything to say about it. "I'm still working out. Plan to pass PT with better numbers than ever."

"Than when you were a fresh-faced rookie? Ha!" Lamont smacked the desk, making the Tupperware jump.

"I will."

"I'll tell you what." Lamont wiped his mouth again. "You top your best record, PT, and marksmanship, then lunch is on me for the rest of the damn year. Otherwise, it's on you."

"Oh, you are on." Brody stuck out his hand.

"And *you* are going to lose." Lamont shook on it.

They finished up lunch, and a heavy silence fell between them. Lamont probably knew he was going to ask, even if he shouldn't. Technically it was his and Griggs's case now, not Brody's. Screw technicalities. It would always be his case until it was solved.

"So..." he began.

"Uh-oh, here we go." Lamont sat back and folded his hands over his chest.

"You know I have to ask."

"I know. And you know, on the record, it's none-ya business. But off the record, I'd like to run a few things by you."

"You fucking better."

"I mean, you have been with the case longer than anyone and..."

"And?"

"Something isn't right. I know you said that when we called on the boyfriend, lover, whatever, and you fucked up your knee, but now there's more to it."

Brody scooted his chair closer, leaning in. "Tell me."

"The labs finally came back on the last vic. Not only no sexual assault, but no assault at all, other than the strangulation marks."

"So why work so hard to make it appear like it was a sexual assault? Skirt torn, underwear gone..."

"Exactly." Lamont rubbed his shaved head. "She was left exposed, but...nothing. No contusions, nothing besides the neck."

"So all of the stuff with scene happened postmortem. Our perp set it all up after Amber was already dead."

"And it's like she didn't even defend herself. We keep chasing these guys they were with, but we know it's not them.

Next we're chasing some mystery assailant that what? Strangles women and then takes the time to make it seem like they were sexually assaulted? It just doesn't..."

"It doesn't jive," Brody agreed.

"No, it doesn't."

"So what do you think?"

"I don't know." Lamont shoved back in his chair. "I know something ain't right, but other than that, I'm still looking. I wanted to let you know. Everyone knows what the case is to you, man. So turn it over in that head of yours and let me know what you come up with. But you *did not* hear shit from me, right? Captain is being weird as hell about the case and...just don't make a stir about it. Think on it. Look over the file if you want, but on the QT."

"I will." Brody nodded. "It'll be good for me. I'm getting back into shape physically, but I have to keep my mind right too. I'll get back here ASAP and keep you from killing Griggs."

"In that case"—Lamont chuckled—"better get back here ASA*F*P."

That was exactly what Brody intended.

CHAPTER ELEVEN

The breeze off the ocean cooled his sweaty skin. Even the constantly complaining seagulls seemed welcoming. The beach was always the best way to end the day, and in Zack's mind, anyone who felt otherwise was freaking nuts.

He jogged past a family strolling and chuckling as their dog attacked the incoming waves. He came to a stop back at the stairs and wiped the sweat from his forehead, sweeping his hair from his face. The late-afternoon sun hung low in the sky, making the water shimmer and giving everything a glow.

He was living the dream.

Well, almost. The only thing missing was Brody's smirk as he raced him back to the stairs. Shoving at each other as Zack laughed, before completely whooping his ass.

Just as well Brody wasn't here, though. He was picking out places for them to train later this week, and bringing him along would've wiped any concentration from his mind. He couldn't focus on making Brody sweat and ache for all the thoughts of getting him home…and making him sweat and ache.

Now *that* was a damn good plan.

His phone vibrated against his thigh, yanking him away from the indulgent mental image, and he froze when he saw the caller ID.

His father.

"Shit."

To say he was surprised was like saying a cow was surprised when hit with a cattle prod.

"Shit. Fire. Damn."

Last time his father had called, it was his birthday. The workings of his mother, no doubt. His father's voice had that chastised, *"He's your son, you can at least call him on the day he was born!"* tone to it.

Zack moved toward the staircase, took a slow, deep breath, and answered. "Hey, Dad."

With his father's, "Hey, Zack," monotone reply, he immediately fell into auto mode. He prepared for the wading-pool depth of conversation that was about to take place and the painful awkward silences that would draw out into infinity. Amazing how quickly he could fall into this mode, able to neglect everything he felt about his father, everything his father made him feel about himself, and instead dance along to the lame-ass tune of a "good son." Everything was "Fine," and "It's great to hear from you," and "Yeah, just working hard. You?"

The artificial sound of his voice left a bad taste in his mouth, but it was a must. Otherwise the thoughts would grow, bigger and bigger until they threatened to crush him. The thoughts he was too chickenshit to ever voice.

I know Mom told you to call me. You remember, the ex-wife you abandoned with a three-year-old son and his two older sisters? Yeah, them, you piece of shit! The family you've completely ignored since the day you walked out. That is, until you need something. I know you're not really interested in talking to me, so drop the act and tell me what you want from *me—because you never wanted me. You don't even know who the hell I am.*

But he'd never say it.

This time was slightly different in that there was no reason to call. No imminent holidays, no birthdays, his father didn't sound physically ill or slightly inebriated. He fought the swell of hope that his inner child fought frantically to keep alive. Maybe his father was really just...calling to say hi.

He barely got the notion through his mind before his dad said, "So my son injured himself playing lacrosse."

Zack froze as his father continued. "Pulled his hamstring. The doctor recommends physical therapy and suggested a place on campus, but I don't even *know* those people. I'd just take him somewhere close to home, but he wants to do it near school. They started him on this regimen and—"

Zack sat down with a *thump* against the stairs and listened to his father's heated tirade of money and college and therapy and lacrosse. A huge, heavy lump settled in his stomach as he listened and interjected with appropriate "mmm-hmms" and "oh reallys?"

But inside, all he heard was, "*My* son." Not once had his father ever referred to Zack as "my son," and Zack knew he never would. Biologically he was every bit the man's kid, but emotionally, they were strangers.

Trent and his not-so-new-anymore wife were his father's family. Not Zack and his sisters and his mom. His new family had somehow earned his attention and affection, while Zack's family had had to fight and silently hope and pray for any kind of interest growing up. Some kind of sign that they were worth his time or even worth a damn.

Zack quickly rattled off a PT he knew from grad school who worked in the area. It was enough to placate his father. A quick "thanks" and "I better go now. Dinner's on the table," and he listened to his father hang up. Fighting everything back, Zack gripped the phone so hard his fingers went numb as a sharp beeping filled his head.

He was rooted to the steps. Pressure rose from the pit of his stomach, up into his throat, choking him. The little flame of hope that had flickered at the start of the call was stamped out. He dropped his head into his hands at his own stupidity. He was nearly thirty and still hadn't learned *not* to expect. *Not* to hope. He'd completed seven years of college, finished with top grades, had a dream job and a pristine practice reputation, yet the concept of not expecting anything from his father was so damn difficult to grasp.

The pressure spread across his chest, down into his arms, pinpricks of fire sparked in his eyes, and his heart began to race. It'd been ages since he'd felt like this, but the familiar rise of nausea and rapid breathing were all too familiar. He blinked. And blinked again. Gripping the phone like he would crush it, he fought the tears burning his eyes. His dad would always be a selfish dickhead. He'd never appreciate or give two shits about Zack. Why couldn't he just accept that fact and move on?

"Fuck." It came out as a deep sob. Holding it back caused his jaw to grind and ache, but he fought it. He ground his teeth as the tears rolled hot.

"*Fuck* this." He stood and shook his head, blinking hard. There was no way in hell he was going to go through this because of his fucking father. Already the attack was imminent, but if he gave in, it was a dive into a nest of deep, dark shit that only reminded him how he wasn't good enough, never would be, and the clincher, he was the world's biggest coward for never telling his father how he felt about him as a dear old dad.

He zipped his phone into his shorts and tightened his shoelaces. He jogged onto the sand, and once he reached the hard-packed stretch near the water, he let loose.

Zack ran. Harder and faster than he had in months. Drawing in long, deep breaths, he pushed and pushed. Thighs burning in protest as he ran toward…something. Or maybe it was away. Fuck if he cared, he just had to keep going, keep moving, or lose himself to panic.

He ran until he felt light-headed, until his legs quivered, until the world around him swirled and tilted and nausea gripped him, this time from exhaustion. He collapsed, landing face-first in the sand. He spat out a mouthful of sand at the epic fail he'd managed not to avoid. As he rolled over onto his back, he was surprised his muscles even let him after the thrashing he gave them. It went beyond the feel-good burn, the rush of endorphins that went with a great workout.

This was a premeditated plummet into oblivion.

Zack stared up at the sky and realized it was dark. How long had he been at it? The lights from the pier shone in the distance, and a breeze held a few notes from an outdoor band. His legs screamed in protest as he reached for his phone and laughed bitterly.

"Mission friggin' accomplished, genius."

He slumped back from the effort, phone in hand. He'd started today's run from his front door and now, smart guy that he was, he'd smashed his ass to the point he could barely move.

The light from his phone's display caused him to squint. It was nearly nine at night. How the hell? He could probably make it home. He'd have to walk, or hobble more like, but his legs weren't broken. Yet.

He really didn't want to. He didn't want to go home to an empty house. Empty rooms he'd fill with all his thoughts and memories, only to feel like shit again.

He did not want to be alone.

His fingers moved across the touch pad before he could doubt himself. *SOS. Half-dead at beach. Come pick me up?*

Seconds later, he got a message back. *I'm assuming this isn't literal, or I'm sending a unit.*

Zack replied with a winky face. It was all he could muster.

A second later. *Folly Beach?*

He shot off a quick *Yep* before he let his head fall back onto the sand.

Brody didn't take long. Zack heard a car pull off to the side of the road near the access and the slam of a heavy car door, some steps in the sand, a fair amount of low cussing about the sand, and then the beam from a flashlight sweeping the beach.

"Zack?" Brody called out. "You okay?"

Zack gave a little wave from his supine position. "Basically." He hadn't moved, and now his ass was getting itchy from the sand. The light blinded him as Brody stood above, the flashlight shining on him from head to toe.

"I've fallen, and I can't get up," Zack said with a smirk.

"You don't look injured or like you've been attacked, so what the fuck happened?" Brody turned off his flashlight, the rising moon creating enough of a glow to see.

"I whipped my own ass."

There was certainly enough light to see the hint of a smile as it crossed Brody's handsome face. Fuck, he dug that smile.

"I needed backup." Zack groaned as he raised himself into a sitting position. "Thanks for coming here." He lifted his hand, preparing to be hauled up. But Brody ignored his hand and instead sat next to him.

He gave Zack an assessing look.

"I didn't realize you were training for the Iron Man. What

the hell are you trying to do out here?"

Zack laughed. It was forced, but it gave him something to do as he dusted the sand off his chest. He knew he had to look like hell.

Brody's face was unreadable as Zack felt the solid weight of his hand resting on his back. Brody was in detective mode. Fine-tooth-comb level looking him over, not missing a damn thing, and Zack knew he had a big neon sign, flashing, *SOMETHING IS WAY WRONG WITH THIS ONE.*

He just wasn't sure Brody wanted to hear about it. He wasn't even sure he wanted to talk about it.

"You sure you're all right?"

Wasn't that the question of the century? Most of the time, yeah, he was all right. His great life was the perfect defense mechanism for coping with the fact he'd been thrown away by someone who was supposed to love him the most. He was okay, just...a little crazy sometimes. Crazy like over the cuckoo's nest or crazy as in just a spaz—that was debatable. But Brody wouldn't want to hear all that.

"Fine, I think," he said instead. "I mean, I'm fine. I am." Brody's gaze darted to his then, eyebrows raised. Not convinced. "You sure about that?" He moved his hand on Zack's back to gently grip his neck, warm and a little sandy. Brody wasn't a touchy-feely guy, so the affection in the gesture warmed Zack to his toes and broke through any bullshit answer he might have come up with.

"I'm not all right. My dad called. He's an asshole. He's always been an asshole."

Brody started rubbing, edge of his hand brushing against Zack's wet hair. "Yeah?"

"I mean, he wasn't violent or a drunk or anything. Not like that. But we—my mom and sisters—were *completely* a waste of time to him. Nothing we did was ever worth his interest. Right up until he decided to make it official and left. He was an emotional void and has been my whole life. He lived at our house, but he merely existed. There was nothing there."

Why was he spilling all this on Brody? The man had enough to deal with, and Zack didn't intend to unload his barge of daddy issues in his lap. Zack clamped his lips shut.

"Where is he now?" Brody asked. The rubbing continued, strong and reassuring.

"With his new and *improved* family," Zack found himself sharing. He didn't want to but couldn't stop. Not with Brody asking in that soothing tone, his hand warm and solid at his back. "Married himself into a nice little two point five kids, designer dog, and a house," he continued. "It'd be okay if that was it and he was the same jackass to them, but—"

Zack's voice caught. He chuckled at his lame story and at what Brody must think. A man who'd probably seen more gruesomeness in his life, people spread all over walls, listening to his sob story of an absent father. He must find it pathetic, but the wound was open now, and there was nothing stopping it. "I know it's a shitty thing to say, but it'd be different if he was the same with his new family as he was with us. But he's not. He's stellar fucking father of the year with them. Just had the rare call from him making sure his 'son' is getting the best for his lacrosse injury. Load of bullshit."

Zack paused in his word vomit to release his fingers from where they were tangled up in the bottom edge of his shorts. Gripping the material so hard his thigh hurt. His heart was racing again, with the reliving and the fact that he was essentially leaving himself bare to Brody in a way he hadn't been.

He turned to make eye contact with Brody and found nothing but quiet interest. Just soothing rubbing at his neck, letting him ramble. He intended to let it stop there. But the snowball had started and— "You know? I'm not a bad guy. I've studied hard, worked my ass off. Gotten a good job, a house. Got good friends, help my mom out at her house. It's not like I'm some deadbeat or anything. I'm not a bad son." Zack took in another breath and let it out. "The man doesn't even know who the hell I am. Nor does he give a shit."

The rubbing at his neck stopped. Zack turned to look at Brody, whose eyes flicked to meet his before looking back at his hand. The rubbing commenced again.

"I know what you mean." Brody's voice was steady but dark, speaking volumes of understanding.

The depth of *something* in his words had Zack reaching out with his hand, finding the firm line of Brody's thigh, fingers brushing over the material of his pants. "Your dad an ass too?"

Brody huffed and shook his head. "No. He was the greatest man I've ever known."

Zack's fingers tightened. *Was...* Oh crap. He was the biggest ass ever. "I'm sorry."

Brody met his eyes then, sincere. "No. It's okay. I miss him, but it was a while ago now. He was far from perfect, so...I get it. My ole man was great, everyone who knew him would probably agree. Minus the criminals, that is. Single parent, managed to retire as a captain, hero of the Charleston Police Department, hero to all. We were really close, but he never knew me either, not the real me. He never knew... Anyway, I know what he would've thought, so I never told him."

Never knew. Knew Brody was gay. Damn. Talk about a defining moment in understanding the inner workings of Detective Douglas Brody. Zack assumed there was more to this than just his dad never knowing.

"You know what he'd think?"

Brody's mouth tightened and the hand stopped, moving to rest in the sand at the base of Zack's spine. "He—" Brody swallowed. "Cops, especially old-school cops, aren't exactly a liberal bunch. Especially during my dad's era, they weren't an accepting crew unless you were cut from the same cloth. I got the big picture early on."

Zack nodded, and they sat in comfortable silence. Except for the whirring in Zack's head. He wanted to know more. Hear the whole thing, but Brody was silent again, and he knew better than to push. He doubted anyone had ever heard this much from Brody. He took it as a compliment.

"I think I have some beer in my fridge." Zack smiled as Brody's face lightened, the darkness fading, replaced with easy amusement.

"Do you mean beer, or is that a euphemism for...?" Brody cocked his eyebrow up again.

"Take me home and find out."

Brody chuckled and patted Zack's back before he stood and

helped Zack up. Zack groaned as every muscle flared in protest. "Fuuuuuuuuuck."

"Beer is one thing, but do you think you're up for *beer?*" Brody looked amused, the heat rising in his eyes as he looked Zack over.

Zack grinned and shoved at Brody as he started climbing the stairs. "I would have to be on my deathbed before I would say no to *beer* with you."

—✳—

Brody followed him into his pitch-black house. "I can't see shit in here," he griped. "Shouldn't you have a lava lamp or something you leave on so you can see?"

Zack stopped short so Brody ran into the back of him. It earned him a playful shove forward.

"Lava lamp? I'm not that boho. They're a fire hazard. Besides, don't cops have super night vision or something?" He flipped on the overhead light and hobbled into the kitchen. "I can see just fine."

"So can I." Brody squinted at the flood of fluorescence. "I just like giving you hell."

Zack grinned to himself as he pulled two Coronas out of the fridge, popped the top off with an opener, and passed one over to Brody.

Brody shook his head, his lips curling into a smile at the beer selection. As he reached for it, his jacket gaped open, the gold shield at his hip catching the kitchen light.

"Whatcha got there, Detective Brody?" Zack pointed, mind suddenly off his sore legs and on the reminder that his current lover was a smoking-hot law enforcement officer who got to wear cool shit like a badge. "Is that your...shield?"

Brody glanced down, tilting his badge up with his free hand. "That'd be it. Won't lie, it's kind of nice to have it on again."

"And I won't lie, this whole badge, gun, handcuff, cop thing? Very hot. Holy shit, do you have handcuffs somewhere on you right now?"

One dark eyebrow eased up.

"There's so much innuendo I could rattle off right now. I'll restrain myself, though." Zack cracked up at Brody's face.

"Okay, seriously. No dirty jokes." Zack took a sip of his beer. "For now. You need a lime for your beer, or can you manage without?" he asked.

"I'll be okay." Brody took a long sip. "What about you? You going to be okay?"

He took another sip. "Yeah. I don't usually go for citrus in my beer, and my sudden onset of cop fetishism may or may not go into remission."

Brody laughed. "Not the beer-and-cop thing. The other stuff. Your dad? You about ran yourself into the sand. Are you better now or still feel the need to self-medicate with overexercising as punishment?"

"Uh-oh. Ding, ding, ding. Someone's finally pegged me for the deflecting mental case I really am." Zack grinned and took another sip. He walked into the living room and, without answering, flipped on a lamp and flopped back on his couch. "I'll be all right," he said eventually, picking at his beer label. "I'm used to my dad taking the wind out of my sails, because he's an asshole that way." He heard the vehemence in his own voice, making the words sound false.

Brody stood by the couch, his gaze full of assessment and clearly not buying what Zack was trying to sell. "You're not a mental case. I've seen *real* nut jobs. You just have baggage to deal with. So does everyone. So do I. Fucking freight train full. But there's a difference between that and dangerous mental issues."

Zack waited for him to finish, but that was it. No coddling. No "*There, there, Zack, you poor boy. You're awesome and perfect as Christmas morning.*" Just a blunt analysis that was so true, it helped lift the tonnage on Zack's shoulders.

He shook off some of the emotional weight. "You're right. I'm sort of normal, I guess. And shit happens. About two or three times a year, I hear from him, and I feel like hell for twenty-four to forty-eight hours, and then I get over it and get on with life. I should be used to it by now." He shrugged. "I'll be okay."

Brody eased down on the sofa beside him, sipping his beer as he slid back. "So you don't need me to stay?"

"Whoa, now." Zack turned halfway around. "I didn't say that. I'm not *that* okay."

Brody smirked over the top of his beer. He took a long draw off the Corona, his neck arched, throat moving with the swallow.

Zack was well aware of the fact he stared every damn time Brody did that, but he couldn't stop. He had a sexy neck, and the way Brody threw his head back was reminiscent of someone in the throes of spectacular sex.

Brody looked over at him, taking in what had to be a blatantly hungry expression all over Zack's face. "What?"

"How attached are you to that beer?"

Brody's eyebrow crept up again. "Why?"

Zack reached over and plucked the beer from his relaxed grasp. He set it on the end table and leaned over, pressing the side of his leg against the thick heat of Brody's quad. He cupped the slightly bristled jaw and brought their mouths together, sinking in, the warmth, the growing familiarity, but the kiss was still different. Not like the mostly one-sided first kiss on the beach, not the hot rush of their desperate make-out session in the hall. This was slow and warm like heat on a knotted muscle. It spread from Zack's mouth down into his chest. He sucked at the plumpness of Brody's lips, taking each one between his lips in turn, ducking a hand under Brody's T-shirt to feel more.

He bumped against something at Brody's side and eased back to look.

Right. That'd be Brody's gun—literal gun, not the pet name for his big cock—hanging close to his side, tucked away, all secure and snug and deadly. Just chilling out near Brody's ribs.

He should've expected it. That was the thing about cops. They usually had guns. Zack wasn't much for firearms, but this one, worn by the right kind of man, didn't bother him. In fact...he did a gut check.

Yep. On Brody, it was a huge turn-on.

He leaned in for another kiss, curving his torso so he didn't bump that gun, fully intending to do more than bump the other one. "Stay here. With me," he whispered, hoping like hell Brody was willing to take that next step.

—✦—

Brody tilted his head back, soaking in Zack's height, the lean and tightly packed muscle, and the fact that his request wasn't so much a question as a demanding plea. Each slick pass of Zack's tongue made him care less and less how he worded anything he said.

"Okay," he managed between kisses.

Zack dragged his mouth along Brody's jaw, sucking at the skin, leveraging his weight farther over him. He slid his leg over and in between, pressing against where Brody ached. Zack's thigh rubbed his; his crotch pushed against Brody's side.

Zack was looming over him. It wasn't subtle, and Brody didn't care. He ran his fingers through the longest part of Zack's hair, threading through and holding on as Zack eased his lips lower and lower. Zack shoved his shirt up, nibbling at the sensitive skin above one hipbone. Brody's body tightened, pushing his hips up and toward Zack's mouth.

Zack unbuttoned his dress pants, caressing Brody's erection through the material. "Lift up your hips."

He did exactly that, trying not to note that every time Zack told him what to do, a thrill skipped across his nerves as he followed orders.

Zack peeled the pants and boxers down to his thighs, his brown eyes shining as he took in the length of Brody, jutting up between them, refusing to be ignored. He leaned up to start loosening Brody's tie, unbuttoning the shirt. "By the way," he said as he worked on getting Brody damn near naked. "You in a suit? Also very hot. But getting you out of this suit? Surface-of-the-sun hot."

Brody dropped his head back on the sofa and allowed himself a small smile. Attention from Zack, being complimented, appreciated for stupid shit like wearing a suit, was a heady combo. It shouldn't affect him. He shouldn't care. But he'd never stuck around long enough for a lot of words. There was never an opportunity for someone to share what they thought about him, or their little kinks. The whole getting-to-know-you part was brand-fucking-new, and there had never been a time he'd done something like this wearing his badge and gun.

Fuck.

His mind started to churn on that fact, turning it over and over and over. Zack was a person he knew and liked, and Brody was wading out, neck-deep into murky, unfamiliar water. What the hell was he thinking? He was sitting here doing exactly what he'd spent years working hard to avoid. *Now* he was going to fuck it all up. Why?

Zack.

The answer was front and center in his brain as much as the man was front and center between his legs. Zack was everything anyone in their right mind would want. He also happened to be another man.

A man who started to use his tongue on Brody's swollen flesh, and everything else began fading away. He forgot to panic. To worry that he wasn't fitting into the dark, sad little box he had created for himself. Where he couldn't have what he wanted. Where he couldn't *be* wanted.

Zack wanted him.

Wanted him here, in his home. *Needed* him in this moment. Brody needed him too. And he could stifle his fucking fucked-up head for one night and be there with someone who actually gave a shit about him. Someone he cared about right back.

Zack gazed up at him, flicking out his tongue to tease the head of Brody's cock. "Take your shirt off," he said, his breath cool on Brody's bared skin. "I want to look at you."

Brody shifted to take off his jacket and unfastened his holster without ever taking his eyes off Zack. Zack made a happy whimpering noise and rocked back on his feet, watching.

"Your door locked?" Brody asked.

Zack nodded.

He slipped off his holster and gun and laid them on the side table. He unbuttoned his shirt as Zack slid his hands up each thigh, helping with the bottom buttons. He ran his large hands, sure and certain, up Brody's chest, through the dusting of hair, and thumbed each nipple on his way back down.

Zack was so relaxed when they were together like this.

Comfortable in his own abilities and going for what he wanted. Brody both reveled in it and envied him. He ran his hands down Brody's thighs, skimming his balls and causing his cock to twitch like it was reaching for contact.

Zack obliged, sinking down onto him with his mouth so hot and wet. The suction, the unabashed desire, had Brody seeing stars. He reached for Zack, tangling his fingers into the long, soft hair, still a little gritty in places from the sand.

A moan escaped as he dropped his head back again, lifting his hips toward Zack's mouth. Zack cupped him, massaging his sac, making it wet by dipping his fingers into his mouth alongside Brody's dick.

"Fuck," Brody groaned. It was desperate and needy. He'd spent so much of today thinking about Zack, his laugh, that ass, his kiss, his wild hand gestures about every fucking thing.

He looked down, and Zack stared right back. He pulled away just long enough to stand and strip off his shirt as well. Entranced, Brody reached for the running shorts and the cut of Zack's hip that led down to what he wanted. He slid the shorts and briefs down, and Zack stepped out of them, straightening so Brody could scan all six foot four inches of his body. The long jut of his cock stood straight up too, showing exactly how much sucking Brody off affected him. Zack grinned beneath a fall of his hair and moved forward, straddling Brody and lowering himself down to rest his ass where Brody ached for him. He kissed down Brody's bare neck, over his Adam's apple, and licked his way back up the left side to suck at the tender area by his ear.

Brody tensed, relaxed, tensed up again—no fucking clue how to react to all the unrushed pleasure Zack doled out. This wasn't a bathroom stall. There was no reason to rush or push things to the end. Zack had his hands all over him; in his hair, down his arms, on his chest, tweaking each nipple. He grew harder, longing for this thing he'd never had until now. Time. Time and so much attention.

Zack took Brody's hands and settled them on his waist. Rocking forward and sliding back, the crack of his ass nuzzled up against Brody's erection, taunting him with a promise. He put his hands on Brody's chest and leaned forward, arching his lower back. "You might be interested to know," he said, voice low, "I woke up hard this morning, just thinking about your chest."

Brody couldn't manage any kind of comeback, just the deep, rapid rhythm of his breathing.

Zack spread his fingers wide over Brody's pecs, curling them in possessively. "That's not all I was thinking about."

Brody swallowed hard, waiting as Zack tilted his hips forward so the tip of Brody's dick was right at Zack's opening.

"I thought about you inside of me too." A rush of hot breath made Brody's brain flicker like a power surge. "I want you to fuck me. Just like this. Fuck me so I can watch you doing it."

Brody swallowed again, blinking, trying to concentrate on not exploding all over Zack's ass before they even got that far. Instead he gripped the hard muscle of Zack's waist and held on as that voice took him apart. His heart skipped with the thrill and fear of it. He liked Zack, but he'd never let someone take over this way, almost in charge, so sensual, involving Brody's mind, all his senses, everything.

The gravelly heat of Zack's voice was laced with all the things he wanted to do to Brody. All he wanted Brody to do to him.

Brody was speechless, his fingers twitching with an ache to do exactly what Zack described, but at the same time, he was rooted to the spot, listening.

Zack moved his ass in a slow motion, hips thrusting gently up and down, rubbing softly against where Brody was so fucking hard, leaking and making it slide, catching on Zack's rim. Each catch had Brody biting down a moan and gripping harder, digging into the hot flesh.

"I've also imagined you on top of me." Zack kept talking, biting at Brody's neck in soft nips. "Gripping my legs, holding me up with those thick, strong arms." He ran his hands up the curves of Brody's biceps.

"I want you to look down at me while I watch your ass move in the mirror." Zack's mouth was back at Brody's ear, his hands moving Brody's to glide down to Zack's round, perfect ass. "I want to feel you pound into me."

Brody brushed his fingers past Zack's opening, and the instantaneous reaction made his cock jump.

"I want you so much." Zack dropped his head forward, breath coming out in little strained pants. "Fuck. I can't think about anything else."

Brody managed to nod again and knew he had to say something. Anything other than sitting there like he was a mute bobblehead doll. He gripped Zack's ass and hauled him forward, Zack's erection digging into his stomach. "I want that too. Right now."

The smile that swept Zack's face was near blinding. "Come on, then." He slid off Brody's lap and held out a hand to help him up.

Brody stepped out of his pants and toed off his shoes and socks to follow. Glancing back, he grabbed his holster and gun and followed Zack down the hall.

"Do I ask?" Zack eyed the weapon in his hand.

"Habit. Don't just leave your weapon lying around."

Zack turned and walked backward in front of him, reaching for him, long limbed, oozing casual confidence even walking fucking backward down a dark hallway. "That's pretty hot, actually. Ever vigilant and all that."

"You think everything is hot."

"Everything involving you."

He wanted to smile. He wanted to fall into the depths of Zack's brown eyes, at once accepting and comforting while still seeking comfort, but he knew that letting himself anywhere near that edge...he'd never come back.

Zack walked into the dark bedroom and flipped on a lamp. The room was like the rest of the house. Eclectic and comfortable, a beach bum kind of look, nothing quite matching, but everything flowed, the look making sense in its spastic ease. Kind of like the man himself.

Zack opened the nightstand drawer and withdrew a foil packet and small tube. He crawled onto the bed, naked, shameless, and strong. He turned to Brody and sat back on his heels, hands loose on his thighs as he waited.

Brody took in the bed; the comforter was all muted shades of blue. Big, fluffy white pillows. Something like what he slept in at home. A bed. He'd never had sex in a bed before. Realization of that fact made his chest ache.

A hand latched on to his wrist and pulled him forward so he half stumbled and fell.

Zack pushed him back and leaned over him, smiling down. "I'll grow old waiting for you to sort all this shit out in your head. I'm horny as fuck, so we're going to save that for later and jump ahead to the good stuff, yeah?" He stroked Brody's cock, because it hadn't lost any of *its* interest.

"Yeah." Brody nodded.

Zack dove in to kiss him. Hot and hungry. No more soft or gentle or slow. He was all tongue, sucking and biting, his sure hands stroking with confidence, thumb catching on the head of Brody's cock, making him suck in a breath. Zack chuckled and pressed a quick kiss before leaning up with a grin. "Up."

Brody scooted back until his head hit a pillow. It felt familiar. And odd. No bathroom-door handle digging into his back or the smell of bleach. It smelled like Zack. Like the ocean and shampoo and man. He watched Zack reach for the lube, moving up to straddle Brody's hips.

"Here." Zack reached for Brody's hand and squirted some of the lube onto his fingers. His grin widened as he leaned over Brody's chest, mouth reaching for his before pulling back to speak against his lips. "I don't know how much you've done, but I'm going to guess it...lacked a lot of the detail I prefer." Zack kissed him again, sucking his lips. "Move your fingers around my ass, press, but don't go in. Make me ache for it."

Brody moved his hand, steadying Zack's hip with the other. He was right. He hadn't done all this before. He felt ridiculous. Thirty-three years old and little to no fucking skill when it came to making it great, making it last, and making it matter. But Zack talking it out, his voice all sex rough and needy, made everything okay. The weight, the burden of his life, it floated away.

He reached between Zack's legs, exploring, gentle, knowing how it felt once before but never having prepped anyone himself. Guys looking to score in a club, drunk or high...yeah... It wasn't about a lot of foreplay. Zack rolled his head back, exposing his throat and tilting his pelvis to help.

"Yeah...that's it." Zack bit at his lip as his hand gripped Brody's shoulder.

Brody felt the tension in Zack's thighs as he rubbed two fingers over the opening, curious more so about what it was doing to Zack. He pressed in, feeling the tightness around the tip of his finger.

"It's okay." Zack's eyes fluttered closed. "Keep going."

He pressed in a little farther, and Zack rocked back against his finger. He knew how it was supposed to go, even if he hadn't done a lot of prepping during the times before. Or even had much anal sex period, making him nowhere near Zack's level, but it wasn't like he'd never watched it. Late at night. Online. He'd gotten off on watching men do this plenty of times.

He didn't want to think about how angry he'd be at himself after. Not here. The tumult of emotions, hating himself for not accepting who he was. It was absurd. He moved his hand back and then forward again, sliding into Zack, wanting the darkness in his head to just go away.

"Fuck yeah." Zack let out a soft groan, digging his fingers into Brody's skin. "Like that. Keep...keep doing that."

So he did. He did exactly what Zack told him to do, because, more than anything, he wanted this to be good for him. Zack had been with men before, not hidden away and hurried, but *with* them. Brody refused to appear the rank amateur he was, and no way in hell would he allow himself not to stack up to Zack's other lovers.

Laughable, because before he'd been too fucking scared to do what he wanted. Take what he needed. But not now. And right now, he needed Zack.

"Yeah," Zack said on an exhale, rocking with Brody's hand. "Add a finger... Damn, I want you deep inside me."

And Brody got a thrill every time Zack talked that way.

"It's okay. You won't hurt me. Yeah, like that."

Brody looked up, and Zack pegged him with a dark, knowing gaze. He leaned forward, pushing himself farther onto Brody's fingers, and kissed him before sitting back up and reaching around behind him to stroke Brody's cock. His gaze never wavered off Brody's, back arched so he could manage both.

"I can't wait to ride you. Till you don't even know your own fucking name."

His cock jumped at Zack's words like he might just go ahead and come now if Zack kept talking that way.

Like he knew Brody wasn't going to last forever, Zack shifted and put his hands on either side of Brody's head.

"Okay." Zack reached for the foil packet. "That's enough dicking around without dicking around." He ripped open the foil with his teeth and rolled the condom down Brody's length.

Brody hissed out a breath from the contact, biting his lip, holding back. This was going to be torture trying not to let go. But he *would* hold off. He wanted to see Zack come first; hard, talking a bunch of nonsense, riding him all the way to the end.

Zack added lube to his fingers and reached around, touching himself, preparing. He held Brody's erection and leaned forward, one hand gripping the headboard, the other keeping him steady. Brody felt the press of Zack's opening at his head and heard the slow exhale of breath from above him.

Brody took it all in. The strain of Zack's thighs, the movement of his abs, the golden skin, the tensing of the curve of his biceps as he held a death grip on the headboard. Brody wanted in. He wanted Zack yesterday. To feel him around him, thrust into him. Make him moan, and have him there the next day to do it again. Brody slid his hand up the warm hard plank of Zack's body, rested it on the swell of a pec, the other on a strong thigh.

Zack lowered himself, brown eyes closed and mouth open. Brody's cock throbbed with each inch of heat and pressure, but he didn't dare move. He let Zack lower himself, settle down on top of him. Once Zack's ass hit his thighs, he gripped on to Zack's thigh with one hand, sliding the other up to Zack's neck.

He didn't have to pull Zack down to his mouth, because Zack opened his eyes and groaned long and hard, leaning down for a quick kiss.

"Fuck, you feel good," he said against Brody's lips. "I knew you would." He began to move, and Brody closed his eyes to think of something, anything not to come with the slightest movement.

He felt Zack pull back and slowly push down onto Brody's cock. Measuring, finding his place until...

"Fuuuuuuck." Zack let his head fall forward, gripping at Brody's chest. "That's it." He rolled his hips, and Brody felt the pressure on the head of his dick as Zack found that spot again. Zack groaned, bending over from the pleasure as he fucked forward again.

"Damn." He slowly opened his eyes, brown almost black with heat. "I've been picturing you exactly like this since the day I met you." He pushed back again. "This and more. Right now, I'm going to ride you, and I want you to fuck me blind. You got it?" Zack moved Brody's hands from his hips to his ass, then reached for the headboard.

Brody held on and thrust up into the tight heat, but to say he was in charge was an absolute lie.

Zack rode *him*.

His forearms strained with pulling himself forward, thighs moved from rocking himself back onto Brody's cock. Brody had never felt so damn wanted, so swept up, or so thoroughly fucked before. It was glorious.

Zack *wanted* him. Moaning with each thrust back, chin tilted up, mouth open, groans and soft "fucks" coming free and easy from his mouth. His abandon, his clear need, tugged Brody along and threw him headfirst into sex so intense, he couldn't speak.

Quick, hard, anonymous fucks in the bathroom at out-of-town bars had nothing on this. And they never would again. He knew Zack; he *liked* Zack. Found him funny as hell and hot and decent. Now he was with him, fucking him, being fucked by him, and he wanted it to blow Zack's mind too.

Brody grabbed hard on to his hips and brought him forward, sliding a hand under, finding where he entered Zack, collecting the leftover slick and spreading it over where Zack was hard and throbbing against his belly. He stroked, rubbed his thumb over the head, and sped up his strokes.

"Oh...my *God*." Zack dropped his hand to Brody's chest and clung on, his hips moving faster. "Yeah," he said, voice shaking. "Just...yeah. Right there."

Brody's balls tightened, thighs quivered. He knew he wasn't far off, but there was no way in hell he was coming before Zack did. He lifted his hips, thrusting up with each movement.

He watched as Zack lost the plot. Spouting off expletives and nonsense. "Oh, Brody. I'm gonna come. I'm gonna—" Zack bucked, his body shoving forward once more, bent over Brody's chest as he pumped hotly into Brody's hand and over his stomach. The headboard groaned where Zack almost pulled the damn thing down on top of them. Brody's chest ached from where Zack's fingers dug into the muscle. But he didn't fucking care.

Zack looked so thoroughly spent, totally debauched. Brody could finally let go.

He drove into the heat, erratic and quick, no rhythm other than the desperate climb toward completion. With Zack talking to him from above, panting his encouragements, his forehead resting on his and hands reaching down to grab at Brody's hips, to bring him closer, deeper, Brody groaned as he came. Hard, his whole body tightening the last few strokes, clinging to Zack before collapsing back onto the pillow.

Zack let his head fall to Brody's neck, breath hot on his skin. There were a few beats of quiet before a tired chuckle tickled his neck.

"Damn, Detective. Now I really won't be able to move tomorrow."

CHAPTER TWELVE

Zack only woke up because his feet were inexplicably cold, and he couldn't seem to fix the situation. He fought with the sheets and blanket in a state of semiconsciousness but still didn't manage to cover more than just his shins.

"Just screw you, then," he mumbled at his bedding.

Wasn't all the bedding's fault. It had gotten pretty knotted and tumbled with the nocturnal activities from the evening before.

He rolled over onto his back with a big grin. *Delicious* nocturnal activities that made his body ache in that perfect way that no workout ever could. Memories of Brody, how he moved, the tightly held control, the potential—it made him want more. All in good time. Getting Brody to finally let go and give in to what he obviously wanted would be like releasing a bull and hoping to keep up, never mind stay on.

Speaking of the hot hard-ass...

Zack eased up to his elbows and did a sweep of his room. Problem number one, the sheet and comforter were on the damn floor, and all he had was a blanket. No wonder his feet were cold. Problem number two, where the hell was Brody?

He got up and slipped on a pair of basketball shorts and his ugly yet comfy slippers before hunting down the detective at large. His legs were stiff, more from the running, less from the fucking, and he stretched in long strides as he went down the hall.

"Hey!" he called out as he neared the kitchen. He smelled coffee. That was promising. "Coffee gooooooood," he said to himself. "Brody!"

No answer. The kitchen was empty, but the little green light shone from the coffeepot, calling to Zack like a siren of caffeine. He poured a big cup, added his favorite vanilla creamer until it looked like a latte, and took his search outside. Surely Brody hadn't left without saying good-bye. Not after last night. Not after yesterday.

That was...to be honest, it'd all been kinds of a huge moment. Not just the next step in sex, but what they'd talked about, what they'd shared. Brody had spent the friggin' night. It was bad form to sneak out.

Plus his suit jacket and shirt were still in the living room.

"Yo!" Zack called out the front door. "Brody?"

"What the hell are you yelling about?" Brody said from out of nowhere, making him jump. He came around the side of the house, wearing his pants and undershirt from yesterday. "You're disturbing the peace. I could hear you yelling all the way outside."

"Then answer, and I can quit. I was concerned about your well-being."

Brody cocked an eyebrow and made a show of looking around Zack's front yard. Two big oaks with low-hanging branches were weighted down by Spanish moss blowing gently in the summer beach breeze, the distant sound of morning beachcombers enjoying the day. Palmetto trees dotted the neighbor's yard; huge clusters of humidity-loving plants and flowers colored the yard, and their car was left with windows down overnight, bikes sitting out in the yard because no one would bother any of it. "Because this is such a rough neighborhood? Threats 'round every corner?"

"I was thinking more about up here." Zack tapped his head. He wasn't an idiot, and he wasn't going to dance around the subject of Brody's issues about who he really was. Why? Because he'd learned the hard way that avoiding a topic only fed it until it grew into a huge, gluttonous beast.

"I'm all good up there. Don't worry, I'm not freaking out." Brody nodded, the slightest color painting his skin. "Last night was..." He took a deep breath.

"Yeah. My thoughts exactly. Just checking, though."

"I see you found the coffee." Brody held out his cup, now empty.

Zack took a sip, his gaze on Brody over the edge of his mug. "It was too tempting to pass up."

Brody shook his head and approached the door. Zack stuck his left arm straight out and against the door frame, blocking Brody's path. "There's a fee for refills."

"I can only imagine." Brody's normally stormy eyes warmed at what he must be imagining.

"A kiss will do for now." Zack leaned forward and pressed his lips to Brody's.

Brody's kiss was hesitant, and he took a quick look around as soon as Zack leaned back.

"Seriously?" Zack looked around as well. He was absolutely going to give him shit about worrying *that* much. He stepped back and set his coffee on the little tiki table by the door.

Brody's face was once again carved with seriousness and doubt.

"Allow me to point out a few things, just in case you missed it," Zack began. "Point one: you're a big-ass guy. Scarier than ninety-nine percent of the people on this island. No one is going to say shit to you if anyone happens to see you kiss a guy. They likely wouldn't say shit if you made out with me at the end of the pier. Which, now that I mention it, sounds like a swell idea. Point two: no one here cares anyway! Have you looked around? I live on what is possibly *the* most laid-back place on the planet. I saw a dude cutting his grass by steering his lawn mower from the side of his golf cart, okay? And no one else looked twice. So if we're at my place and I want to kiss you, dammit, I'm kissing you. And you better not ever shy away from me. We got it?"

Brody blinked at him, coffee cup in front of him. He worked his jaw, then finally: "Fine. I get what you're saying, I do. You live at a very chill beach and can do whatever you want, and believe me, I'm envious. But this is a big fucking deal for me, so don't be an asshole about it. Okay?"

"Okay. Fair enough. But don't be all closeted and self-conscious when we're right here in the cone of safety of my house. You weren't last night, inside or outside. Just don't...do that. It's guaranteed to wig me out. Cool?"

"Cool."

"Good." Zack grabbed Brody by his free arm and hauled him forward as he stepped out. Their mouths crashed together when they met in the middle. He slid his fingers into Brody's thick, short hair and tilted his head so he could properly debauch the man the way he ought to be debauched every morning. This time, Brody didn't fight him.

Zack pushed his tongue inside, the kiss warm, tasting of vanilla and dark roast coffee. He could wake up like this on any given day and be just fine. Brody found his waist with his free hand and ran his fingers over the skin, pulling him closer until he reached the dip of Zack's spine. Gooseflesh spread over him, even on the balmy summer morning.

"Better?" Brody asked, his lips a well-kissed pink within the stubble darkening his jaw.

"*So* much better."

"Good. Now move so I can get more coffee; I've got to ask you something."

He stepped aside and let Brody pour another cup. "Uh-oh. This sounds ominous."

"No, I just want to show you something."

He followed Brody around the side of the house to the open backyard that butted up against a neighbor's wooden fence. "Is this really us just slipping around back so we can have sex outside? Because if so, count me in."

"You have no shame. You know, I've arrested people for exactly that."

Zack laughed at the deadpan sincerity in Brody's voice, and some coffee went up his nose. The man wasn't kidding, but it was freaking hilarious. He glanced over at Brody, who was grinning slightly.

"Are you kidding or not? I can't always tell. You're like a flat line on what you give off sometimes."

"No, I'm not kidding, but it is funny. I've probably caught..." Brody stopped walking and looked up at the tree branches, evidently doing math in his head. "Damn, at least ten couples in the act. Calls on strange cars, and we'd show up to find a couple, sometimes married, just having a little quality time in the sedan. Parked at the end of some street, in the empty parking lot of a business, construction site, their own backyard, you name it. People especially like to get freaky in cars."

Zack laughed again. "It is good times."

Brody just shook his head. "Anyway, this." He pointed to a tarp hanging five feet off the ground. "This is what I wanted to show you."

"It's a tarp," he said.

"I know it's a fucking tarp, I mean what's underneath it."

"Oh, my boat?"

"'Oh, my boat,' he says, like everyone has a sailboat in their backyard. Yeah, your boat. I peeked. I didn't know you sailed."

"Well, I don't." Because who the hell was he going to sail with? He wasn't about to sail alone. "Not right now. She's just my never-ending pet project. Why? Don't tell me you sail." He tried to keep the hope from his voice. It was one thing to have Brody in his bed. What he wanted, no matter how unlikely, was Brody in his life.

"I might."

"Detective Brody." Zack put his hand on his heart with dramatic flair, hoping it covered for the fact it'd just lurched with possibility. "I just knew you were a seaman."

"Do you ever stop?" Brody shook his head, the slightest pink to his cheeks.

There was no way he'd stop any time soon if it meant extra time with Brody and making him blush even a little. He might pause it temporarily, but he couldn't stop flirting with the man now that he'd started. Like...ever.

"No, I'm not a seaman. I don't know how to do any of that shit, but I do like being out on the water. Lakes, rivers, oceans, whatever. It's relaxing, and there's no one in my immediate vicinity committing crimes."

"Oh. That makes sense. Allow me to introduce you, then. Here." He handed Brody his coffee cup and grabbed the tarp, folding it back neatly to reveal a small white sailboat. "This is my sloop, *Mystic Mary*. *Mary*, this is Brody. Brody, *Mary*."

Brody stuck the coffee mug back in his hand. "You're not far from being finished."

"Nope. I was going to work on her today and tomorrow, since I'm off. Probably finish her up soon."

"Get her in the water?"

"Only if you'll go with me."

Brody's gaze shot to his as he went perfectly still.

"You said you liked being out on the water, and I don't like being out there alone. Seems like a simple solution." And hopefully it didn't sound desperate.

"I thought you boat people liked being all alone and at one with the sea?"

"First of all, I am not *you* boat people. I am you beach people. We be a social people. Second, what if I get swept out to sea? Third, what if I capsize? Or a pop-up storm hits me and I'm out there all alone? Or a great white shark sweeps in. No thanks." He shook his head. "I believe in the buddy system."

Brody just looked at him, biting back a smile. "You seriously worry about all that? None of that is going to happen."

"Says he who won't even kiss me in my front yard? Your arm get sore from throwing stones?"

"Screw you."

"Okay. But friends don't let friends sail alone. I'll take her in the water, but only if you'll go with."

"Is that what we are, then? Friends?"

Zack studied the man across from him over the top of the boat. Brody had propped his thick forearms on the side, and Zack could see the ropelike veins standing out against hard muscle, making him want to lick and nibble his way up Brody's arms and then, oh say, pin those arms over his head and have his way with him.

"No." Zack laughed. "I'm not sure what I'd call it yet, but my thoughts on you are way too pervy to be friendship."

Brody cracked up. "Well, hell. At least you're honest about it. Come on, then." He started pulling the tarp the rest of the way off *Mary*.

Zack lurched closer to him. "Uhm...whatcha doin'?"

"I'm going to help you finish. With both of us working, we

could finish today, be in the water by next weekend, right?"

"Uh, yeah. You do know it's going to be, like, ninety million degrees today, right?"

He got the eyebrow again. "Ninety million?"

"In the shade." He nodded.

"Then we better get going and be done by the afternoon."

Zack scrunched his face, watching Brody check out the tins of sealant and paint. The man was dead serious. He was going to help Zack finish his boat. Who did that? It was dirty, nasty, thankless work. "You don't have to do all this to get me in bed again," Zack told him. "I'd go willingly if you so much as wiggle your ass. I mean, I'm pretty much a sure thing at this point unless you really piss me off or kick me to the curb, so manual labor isn't required. Just saying."

Brody straightened and stepped closer to him. He grabbed Zack's forearm with one hand and dragged him over to the wooden table. "Quit talking bullshit and tell me what goes on next. I've got time off too, nowhere else to be, and I don't feel like hanging out alone all day with my mind. If you feel me."

"Ahhhh." He stared at Brody a second longer. His dark hair shining in the dappled sunlight, his face pure serious as he studied a menagerie of brushes. "I know exactly what you mean," Zack finally said. "Let me get you something to wear, though, because you'll ruin those clothes."

Thirty minutes later they were painting away, halfway through a coat of paint and drenched in sweat.

"Why *Mary*?" Brody asked as he worked on the starboard side.

"Huh?"

"Why did you name your boat *Mystic Mary*?"

"Oh. Mystic is for the Van Morrison song, 'Into the Mystic.' Song is freaking awesome. Mary is because of Jimmy Hendrix."

He heard the silence of Brody's brush. "Of course it is."

"Hey!"

"No, no—it's cool. It's a good name. I like Morrison. And *some* Hendrix. Damn, it's hot out here."

"Told ya. Ninety *million* degrees."

Brody put his brush down and stripped off the old Cooper River Bridge Run T-shirt that Zack had lent him. "You mind?" he asked, referring to him going shirtless.

Zack couldn't help but cackle. "You did *not* just ask me that. No, I do not mind if you get less dressed in front of me, Brody. Matter of fact, what about with every layer we put on the boat, you take off a layer of clothing. That's *real* motivation."

Brody just shook his head and smirked. He leaned over, painting near the bow of the boat, and Zack finally got a good look at what he'd barely touched the other day. The scar. It ran from just below the top of his left shoulder, slightly down and diagonal toward his underarm. It was lighter than the rest of his skin, slightly raised, and probably years old.

"What happened?" he asked, waiting for Brody to lift his gaze. "On your shoulder, I mean."

"Oh that?" Brody replied without pause or so much as a glance up. "Happened on the job." He kept right on working, no hint of any details.

"Aaaaand?" Zack prompted, refusing to let the stoic routine work. "I say again, what happened?"

Brody stopped painting and sighed. "A knife happened. The vest we wear under the uniform doesn't cover but so much and...shit happens."

Zack waited, but nothing else was forthcoming. He sighed as well, staring at the top of the dark head until Brody finally looked up.

"What?"

Zack raised his eyebrows and waited. "I can stand here like this all day if that's what it takes, but you're not going to leave this topic with *shit happens.*"

"Okay, fine." Brody laid the brush on the upside-down hull. "You won't want to know the details once you do, but fine. We're doing the Q-and-A thing. I get it. It was about five or six years ago. I was finishing up as a uni, already took the detective's exam, and waiting on a position. We get a call about a domestic disturbance. Domestic calls go bat-shit crazy the majority of the time, so we roll up prepared for the worst and that's exactly what we got.

"Some man yelling his head off inside the house. We get in, and he's standing there, fucking huge. Like NFL-offensive-line massive, big knife in his hand. Woman at his feet, we presume the wife. She's bleeding out and there are two kids screaming from the hallway. Father of the year is swinging wide with the knife, right toward the kids. I've got my gun drawn, but all I'm thinking is shit, the kids are too close. And I don't have a clean shot unless I want to hit them. He's either methed out or cracked out of his skull. We try talking him down. Put the knife down, etcetera. He isn't hearing any of it. Will, my partner at the time, decides to go Taser. It's a good call. Except it does next to nothing, because the man is jacked higher than a sky rise. He turns toward me, and I should've shot him, but I didn't trust it, not in that small space with kids a foot or two away. He turns toward the hall again, and his kids were *right there*. So…I jump him. Full weight, I grab him and fall back. We roll. He's built like a fucking water buffalo, and I'm trying to wrestle him. Badly.

"I feel this sharp pain and heat down my shoulder. I know he's at least nicked me with the damn knife. Fucker. I manage to get on top of him. Will is there, trying to pin his legs, and I'm yelling for the kids to get back. It's all we can do to hold him down, and the fucking cuffs won't even fit him, he's that damn big. EMS shows up. Our backup.

"It's chaos.

"Will and backup get the buffalo zip-tied and out the door. I'm worn out, EMS is working on the woman, and the kids are a wreck. I get them together and tell them EMS is going to take care of Mommy. She'll be okay.

"They finally quit crying because they see Mommy being taken care of, and one of them is like, 'Hey, mister. You're bleeding on the carpet.' I look, and it's like a river down my arm. Son of a bitch flayed me open from here to here. But…y'know, better me than those kids.

"Anyway, the mom made it. Kids were okay. Fucking miracle. The guy is still doing time for knocking over a convenience store earlier that night. He stabbed the clerk, took a bunch of cash, and ran. Turns out he got home with the money, and the wife starts raising hell, wanting him out and threatening to call the cops.

"So there ya go. That's my scar story. Want to hear how I blew out my knee and needed ACL surgery?" Brody stood there, having told it all without pausing or even seeming to take a breath.

Zack blinked over at him, his skin prickly and cool. Brody had wrestled with a huge, knife-wielding maniac to save some kids. He told the story like it was just a thing. Like that was what he did all the time. But now, knowing him, knowing stuff like he drank his coffee with creamer too, wore boxer briefs in white only, and listened to Van Morrison—it suddenly meant...more. Brody put himself in danger, real danger. Knife-wielding danger. Every damn day.

"I know how you hurt your knee," Zack finally managed to say. "It was in the patient file from the department. You were on the Strangler case at the time. Is that why you work even harder to get back? I know you love the job, but also...it's a big case. Even I've heard about it."

Brody only nodded, the shutters closing in his eyes. He picked the paintbrush back up and painted in silence. Zack knew when a topic hit a nerve and wasn't supposed to be niggled. He let it go, and they finished the job in comfortable silence.

"I fucking stink," Zack finally said after what seemed like an eternity. The boat was pretty much done, and they'd both probably lost two pounds to sweating.

"Yeah, you do," Brody agreed, swiping at his forehead.

Zack popped him with the shirt he'd taken off. Brody was quick, and it only caught the edge of his ass. Which gave Zack so many thoughts.

"You can get cleaned up here, and we'll go grab something to eat."

"Are you asking me on a date, or just telling me what we're doing next?"

"I'm hungry. You can go home and make a ham sandwich if you want, but I want a shower and then a damn pizza the size of this boat. You in, yes or no?"

"Yes. Hell. I'm going."

"Hey!" Zack called out, making him stop and look back. "I know you aren't used to...you know, letting people in. Outside of work, I mean. So, thanks. Thanks for sharing. A little."

Brody narrowed his eyes, and Zack gave him his biggest grin. He was goading him. Guilty. But Brody reacted exactly how he'd hoped.

He grabbed Zack, trying to lock him around the neck but not trying very hard. Zack slid free easily, slick with sweat. Brody shoved him back, smirking. "You're just asking for an ass kicking, aren't you?" he asked, a new hint of playfulness in his voice.

"Pretty much." Zack smiled.

He followed Brody inside, right behind him, watching him go. The borrowed basketball shorts were slightly too small for Brody's thicker frame. Zack wasn't complaining. Thin material pulled tightly across an ass like that of a Greco-Roman sculpture was a good look. Sure, he was hungry enough to devour a pizza all by himself, but now there was a different hunger that demanded his complete attention.

Thinking about Brody in his day-to-day work, the discipline it took to get the job done, the sharp mind and keen reflexes—knowing how strong and confident Brody could be—it all made Zack want to climb the man like a damn tree. He'd even gotten to imagine Brody in his patrol uniform. Well aware that he was quickly becoming a huge Brody fan boy, he needed to ease up.

He ought to back off, cool his jets a bit. It'd be wise to remember that his new favorite detective was locked in the closet and hiding behind the racks. No matter how much Zack enjoyed this being something smolderingly hot and most likely mutually exclusive...he was in an entirely different place in his life. He could make this a thing. A real thing. But Brody wasn't there and may never get to the point where he could be honest with himself, never mind anyone else.

It'd taken Zack years to get back here, to recover from Marcus. He couldn't torch it all now. This...thing they were doing, him and Brody, it was flaming hot and...fuck, he could get used to having a man like him around. In his life.

But that wasn't what this was. He *should* end it soon. Wise up and think survival. No more Brody. Cold turkey. But he knew he wasn't going to.

Brody turned to him, Zack's gaze catching the scar from the knife wound. He took in the sight of Brody sliding off the borrowed shorts, a quick smirk before walking into Zack's bathroom butt-ass naked.

No. No way could he go cold turkey off Brody. Not yet anyway.

He gave Brody all of about two minutes to get the shower hot and ready, and then he walked into the steam-filled room and stripped down as well.

Brody didn't say a word as Zack opened the shower door and stepped inside with him.

"Good thing I remodeled and made it roomy, huh?" he asked.

Still, Brody said nothing. Only moved over a bit to share the spray of hot water. His eyes were somehow different. Darker again from remembering the past. Zack could only imagine all that Brody had seen, and half of it he didn't want to.

Instead he grabbed the bottle of shampoo and did one thing he knew he could. He gave Brody his undivided attention and the same comfort he'd been given the night before. Silently, Brody lowered his head and allowed Zack to work his fingers through the short, thick hair. He massaged, at first gently, then with increasing pressure, seeing the slump in Brody's shoulders as he relaxed.

They smelled like sunshine, sweat, and salt air. Slowly it gave way to something fruity and whatever the hell else was in his shampoo, but the warm smell of sun remained.

He tilted Brody's head back and stepped in, urging him back under the rush of water. He rinsed the suds from his hair and then grabbed the soap to lather up his broad chest. As Brody moved to help, Zack slapped his hand out of the way but didn't say anything. He'd be damned if Brody was going to deny him the joy of spreading his attention all over that chest.

There was just a rumble of humor and approval from Brody, as if he knew what Zack was thinking. It wasn't until he was satisfied with his work that he lowered his mouth to Brody's and kissed him, long and slow. Slipping his tongue inside, he tasted, explored. He took his time, wanting to remember everything about Brody's kiss, his taste. Burn it onto his brain.

He kissed Brody until he drew a soul-deep sigh and shudder from him. The stiff length of Brody's cock brushed against his, and Zack kissed him harder. He turned and positioned them so the backs of Brody's knees hit the small seat built into the shower. Zack slipped a hand down and ran it once, twice, along the length of Brody's cock before bringing them together, using his own erection to rub against him.

Brody's breathing paused, held before he took another quick inhale.

"*Zack*," he barely whispered. "Damn, you feel good." He leaned one hand on the side of the shower and let his head fall back. He looked like...like in that moment he'd let Zack do whatever the hell he wanted.

Which was good, because there was so much Zack wanted to do...

The suds slicked, foaming up as Zack stroked them together, his hand providing a tight grip to thrust into as their cocks slid next to each.

Brody drew in a shaky breath, letting his head rest back again the tiles. What he was doing? Nowhere *near* enough to get them off. But it felt good.

He urged Brody to sit and allowed himself the moment to take in the sight before him. Brody. Wet, naked, and hard in his shower. He was never going to look at that seat again and not see Brody's form sprawled on it. He was so gorgeous, Zack would maybe even consider leaving it as shrine to the perfection of his ass. The long column of Brody's neck was exposed, eyes closed, mouth open. Broad shoulders and chest flushed red from the heat and arousal, strong thighs spread, cock heavy and hot in Zack's hand.

A cock that he really wanted in his mouth.

Zack watched the changes in Brody's face as he circled a thumb over the reddened head. Watched as his breathing sped up with each pulse of his cock in Zack's hand, his eyes opening and locking on to Zack's. Gray, focused, and deep with want.

Damn.

Zack leaned in and took Brody's mouth quickly before letting him go and reaching out to get a towel. He folded it and dropped it to the floor. Zack knelt down on the wet fabric, resting his arms on Brody's thighs.

Brody let out a loud groan as Zack took him into his mouth, hands flying into Zack's wet hair as he swallowed him in deep, sucking hard. Clean and fresh from the shower, leaving a taste of pure Brody on his tongue. It was addictive.

Zack got into a rhythm, hands rubbing Brody's thighs. He wasn't into speeding things up as long as his legs held, but definitely into making Brody fall apart. Zack cupped and stroked Brody's balls. The soft, delicate skin in his hand made him want to taste more. He pulled back to suck at the tip before letting Brody's dick twitch from his mouth. His hand replaced his mouth, continuing to stroke, firm and slow, as Zack bent to lick at his sac, gently sucking each ball into his mouth. He was rewarded with Brody swearing tightly, ass shifting about, trying to lift his hips into the strokes from his place on the seat.

With his free hand, he gently lifted Brody's balls and swept his tongue against the sensitive place behind them. Brody's sitting position made it awkward, but Zack could skim the area. With each brush, Brody thrust up into his hand. Zack strained his tongue, placing pressure against the area, but it wasn't quite enough. Brody must have also gotten frustrated with the lack of access, because he shifted, lifting his thigh, opening up to Zack. The move itself sent a surge of lust to Zack's dick, and he groaned against Brody's heated skin, using his tongue to lick and press.

He dug his fingers into the muscle of Brody's thighs, getting high on the taste of the freshly washed skin. He strained farther, sliding the tip of his tongue back and grazing the puckered opening. The response was instantaneous. Brody's groan lowered an entire octave and his hands that had been threading through Zack's hair dropped to the back of Zack's neck, pinning him there.

Damn. Like he'd leave?

But if he was going to properly show Brody exactly how good it could be, he needed better access. Zack sat back on his knees, giving Brody's cock one more good-bye suck before patting him on the thighs.

"Okay. Up. Turn around."

Brody nodded, got up, and turned to lean against the shower wall, hands braced above the seat, basically presenting his ass to Zack like it was the world's best gift. And in Zack's opinion, it was.

He'd fantasized long enough about this ass, and now it felt like he had the VIP access pass to the best place on earth. He kneaded the cheeks, and with each rub, he slowly parted them, revealing Brody with each circle.

Zack leaned up and pressed a sucking kiss to the top of the crack. Brody shifted on his feet but remained otherwise still. Zack sucked lower, pressing his tongue between the cheeks, dragging down a fraction before pulling back. The next time Zack sucked at Brody's skin, he parted the cheeks and gently ran the tip of his tongue over the opening.

"Fuck, *Zack*." The voice was low and strained. Brody's legs wobbled, hands attempting to find purchase on the cool tiles.

Zack returned his tongue and pressed against Brody's opening, feeling it twitch. He gave it a few little licks before settling in and stroking his tongue over Brody's hole, circling it, giving little presses to feel it loosen, relax under his tongue.

That was when the occasional curse from Brody changed to full-out groans. Deep, low, and desperate. Brody pushed back with his hands, pressing his ass closer to Zack's face. Each pass had Brody shifting on his feet, as if debating between remaining upright or getting closer to Zack's mouth.

"Touch yourself," Zack whispered against his skin. Brody shifted to lean on one hand, jerking himself off like he'd forgotten he could.

The noises Brody made before were quiet in comparison to the groans he made with every firmer press of Zack's tongue. When Zack felt it give enough that he could push the tip farther inside, Brody shuddered against him. Stuttering in jerking off and almost losing rhythm.

"Fuck, Zack." His moans were a plea. The sweetest pleas Zack had ever heard. "I'm... I'm gonna—"

Zack raised his hand, bringing a finger to breach Brody, the tip sliding in next to his tongue. Sliding out and gathering spit, and slowly pushing in. A little bit more with each lick, until Zack could curl down and—

"Oh. Fuuuuuuuck." Brody jolted as Zack hit what he was after. "Oh fuck, Zack. Zack. Just... Do that again."

Zack smiled against his skin and slowly pressed again, this time licking around the rim, around his finger, as he continued to stroke inside.

Brody came with a shudder and a long moan. Body jerking with each pull, curled in on himself as he splashed hot and wet against the tiles. When the trembling stopped and Brody's legs almost gave way, Zack moved to turn Brody so he could rest against the seat again.

He looked thoroughly debauched, like Zack had fucked him six ways from Sunday. A very, *very* good look and enough to help Zack come. Zack stood up, running his face through the shower, wiping at his mouth and bending to take Brody's. He did his best to straddle Brody's lap and grabbed at his straining cock, pulling hard and quick. He wasn't going to last long, not with the vision of what they'd just done still burning bright in his mind.

Zack groaned against Brody's mouth, which seemed to pull Brody out of his postorgasm haze. Strong hands flew to Zack's neck to pull his mouth closer and harder against him, the other batting Zack's hand away to jerk him off. Quick and brutal and with Brody clinging to his mouth, murmuring encouragements to come. Zack let go and pulsed over Brody's hand, breathing hard into his mouth.

After a few beats, while they attempted to regain their breath, Zack chuckled into Brody's hair.

"Good God, I'm ordering myself two pizzas now. Carbs be damned."

Brody's response was to wrap his arms over Zack's hips and hold him tight. "Mmmm. Two. Each."

CHAPTER THIRTEEN

Brody breathed in the humid, salty, marsh stink of downtown Charleston's air as he and Lamont stepped out onto the sidewalk after lunch. "I'm just glad to be outside the office."

"Making you crazy?"

"Bat shit."

"It's good to be out with you, man. Walking the streets. It's like old times."

Brody smirked. "Old times? I haven't been gone that long."

Lamont scrubbed a hand over his head. "A lot can happen in a couple of months."

Hell yeah, it could. His mind drifted back to the other day. Hanging out with Zack and then in the shower. How it felt, what it made him feel *and* think. Damn. To think a couple of months ago he hadn't even known Zack. Now...

He shook it off. It wasn't the time or place to think about Zack. "So what's new with the case, 'Mont? What do we know?"

"Not a lot more." Lamont strolled along beside him as they headed down King Street through what used to be a bad area, but thanks to its proximity to the university, it'd been revitalized—which was code for small, overpriced studio apartments for the young, wealthy, and childless, and lots of trendy eateries.

"The media is having a field day with it at this point, as I'm sure you've seen. Two murders right downtown in one summer and Captain looks like he's going to pop a vein any day now. The Strangler is escalating, and people are starting to freak out. The shooting the other night down off Meeting?"

"Yeah."

"A grad student packing a handgun. Some guy runs up to tell her she left her headlights on, and she pops him."

Brody shook his head.

"Luckily she wasn't a good shot. Got his arm, but he'll live."

"Unlike Amber."

Lamont slowed his steps and looked around. "Let's hang a left here and keep walking. I need the exercise. Felicia's on my ass about losing weight."

Brody chuckled and followed his partner. Lamont was a massive guy, but he wasn't what you'd call fat. Felicia just preferred the Lamont from his college football days.

"You could start running with me," Brody offered without thinking. And what? Run with him and his gay lover? Sure, Lamont would be jumping at that opportunity.

"What, like that half-marathon bullshit? Hell, no. Unless there's a grizzly bear or a zombie on my ass, I'm not running farther than a few blocks and only then if I'm chasing a perp. Here, let's go this way."

"So the latest girl, Amber." Brody got back on topic and away from his hasty invite. "She have a boyfriend? We looking at him?" He added a snort.

"Nah. No boyfriend. And why do you do that to yourself? You memorize all their names so they can haunt you? You gotta stop that."

"I can't," Brody confessed. It was a damn big confession coming from him, but this was Lamont. It was okay. "You know I can't. Not with this case."

Lamont nodded. "Yeah. I know. Anyway... Captain is off of that boyfriend angle for now. I just don't get it. Why didn't any of them fight their attacker? This last vic —sorry, Amber—was on the girls' track team. She looked strong, fast. I know we said they must know the assailant, but that doesn't fit. How sneaky a motherfucker do you have to be to move in so fast they don't even fight?"

"Very," Brody answered as they hung a right.

When they reached the intersection of Calhoun Street, he knew where they were going, but he didn't say a word.

"What about Griggs, what's he think?" he asked instead.

"Not a damn thing that makes sense. I ditch him for lunch, and he doesn't even clue in to that. It's like he doesn't know I don't like his ass." Lamont shook his head. "How he made detective, much less in Homicide, I'll never know."

Brody snorted a laugh. "Yeah, you do. He's the chief's nephew by marriage."

"The hell you say!"

"You didn't know?"

"No. Sonuva... Well, that explains everything."

"Don't it? Keep looking; keep asking. You know somebody saw something. They had to."

"Yeah, a bunch of overprivileged, drunk college kids like last time. They're proving about as likely to come forward as someone in the projects. Swear I just want to shake the shit out of them every time they start talking."

"Try it. I've seen you use more questionable methods."

Lamont's booming laugh filled the street. "Yeah, on pimps and dealers maybe. Can't you see me shoving some Richie Rich kid nose first against the wall, barking at him to start talking? Mommy and Daddy would be in front of the captain so fast it'd cause a hurricane."

Brody chuckled too, because it was true.

They got closer to the block where the last victim was found, and Brody looked over at Lamont, waiting for it.

"I guess you know where I'm bringing you," Lamont said, slowing as they neared the courtyard of the rental home. Yellow tape still draped the wrought iron fence.

"I knew as soon as we left Meeting Street."

"Look, I want you to check the scene with me, but...there's...there's a caveat. I've paced around here, and now I need your eyes. Griggs ain't got shit on you. We're a good team because we see things differently. I want the job done, and I do my best work with you."

"As do I."

Lamont tilted his head to the side. "I can't believe you finally acknowledged that shit. You feeling okay?" He reached out like he was going to feel Brody's forehead for a fever.

"Get the fuck out of here and get to the point. There's a caveat. What is it?"

His partner widened his stance, put one hand on his hip; the other he used to scrub across his shaved head. This was not a good sign.

"I didn't want to say anything, but..."

"Lamont," Brody growled. "But what?"

"Captain said he doesn't want you anywhere near this case right now."

"*What?*"

"He said we're going to catch the asshole, but he wants fresh eyes on it. Specifically *not yours*."

"What the hell?"

"I don't even know. Probably political bullshit, but he wants no chance of any attorney being able to say a cop who was off duty was messing in it."

"I'm not off duty."

"Light duty, whatever. They don't care. You're not officially on the case anymore, so you can't officially say shit. I'm not even supposed to be telling you this, but like I'm not going to? They can kiss my black ass. You're welcome to look around; hell, go through my files till you can't get enough. I *want* you to, but keep it quiet, and if you find something, it's got to go through me. Not only does Captain Hill not want to hear it from anyone but me and Griggs, but if he finds out I'm giving you guided tours, it's my ass in a sling too."

Brody leaned back against a brick building probably as old as the union, and crossed his arms. "Fucking-A."

"Pretty much."

He looked up and down the sidewalk, empty of any tourists and very few cars, and all he could see was a college girl, walking home alone on a Thursday night, with no idea it'd be her last. A girl who should've been safe. A girl who maybe *would've* been safe if he'd been on the case the last two months.

Guilt gnawed at the edge of his mind. This was his case. It would always be his case. From when he was a rookie so new he squeaked, right up until now. These girls were his responsibility.

"Captain does realize I'm back next week, right?" he asked. "I take my PT testing in a few days. What the fuck?"

Lamont shrugged. "I'm just telling you what he said, not saying I agree with him."

"Fuck them, then." He shoved off the building. He wasn't going to not work this case because Captain Hill was playing favorites. "I'll tell you what I see, what I think."

Lamont just stared at him. "And you'll go hands-off on what you find, right? You can't be officially active in this case anyway. You were never here with me."

Brody stared at his partner. If it was what he had to say to keep Lamont in the clear, he'd live with it. "Sure. I won't do a damn thing but tell you and then sit on my hands. Besides, I *might* have come by here of my own free will while on light duty."

Lamont grinned his perfect, bright, you're-so-full-of-shit smile.

Brody shrugged, the best he could do to reassure Lamont he'd play politics. "I don't want us finding another girl next month, so yeah, I'll play by the rules and be a good boy."

His partner laughed and reached for the yellow tape to lift it up. "And hell will surely freeze over. C'mon. Let's look around."

—✦—

Brody slid farther down in the booth, the worn leather squeaking enough that one of the bar patrons turned to look. He fought the urge to flip the guy off.

But it wasn't that poor throwback hippy's fault he'd had a shit day.

Investigating another dead girl, and the game had definitely changed. The Strangler never struck this close together. Two within three months. There could be another next month if they didn't find the fucker, *and* the higher-ups didn't want him involved.

Fuck that.

The Strangler. It'd been his focus all day and, as always, never failed to leave him frayed at the edges. It had to be someone the girls knew or someone damn stealthy and strong. It didn't point to a reckless youth or young man looking to get his rocks off by exposing women to look like they'd been raped. That sort of motivation didn't lend itself to patience and stealth. So perhaps it was a guy they all knew who was strong enough to subdue them immediately. To the point none of the victims even had DNA under their nails from trying to claw at the attacker.

"Shit," Brody growled, rubbing at his tired eyes before downing the rest of his whiskey. He held up his finger so the waitress would bring him another. Self-medicating. It was better than popping pills, and he didn't drink often. Which was more than most cops could say.

"Here ya go." The perky brunette delivered another whiskey in record time, flashing him a smile. "You just move to Folly or here on vacation?"

Brody looked up at her. She was a beach-bronzed beauty, there was no denying that. Nice body, great hair, amazing smile. And she did absolutely nothing for him. "Neither. Why?"

She smiled again, adding a flirtatious flip of her hair. "We normally just get regulars here, and I know I've never seen you before. I'd remember you."

He stared at her. "Thanks. I'm just here…" What? Why was he here? He didn't live on Folly. He lived fifteen minutes away, at least, and had plenty of bars near his house, a few that knew him. He'd dragged his sorry ass all the way out here to drink himself loose…to be near Zack. Not here *with* Zack. Just near him. Pretty fucking pathetic, but he couldn't go straight from dealing with death to touching Zack

But sitting here, with the warm honey-wood bench and seats, the same color as Zack's stupid, gorgeous hair. And the crazy art on the walls, a wobbling hula girl on the bar. It all just reminded him of Zack. Silly, grinning, fucking perfect Zack.

It wasn't him, but it made Brody feel like he was close.

"I'm here to see a friend," he finally answered before downing half his drink.

"Oh yeah? Who?"

"You islanders are nosy as hell." He shot her a look.

"Sorry." She gave him a glare right back. "Just making conversation. Whoever they are, I'd say they're lucky, so long as you don't bite their damn head off." She gave him another smile, sharp and defensive, before sashaying away.

Brody grimaced. He'd have to leave her a good tip, because he'd just been a jackass. There was no reason for it. Wasn't her fault. He wasn't mad at the cute bar girl or the old beach bum. He was mad at himself. For another dead girl added to this case, for even entertaining the idea that he might not get his case back after he returned, and for the fact that he was this close to Zack and still hadn't called him.

It was a creepy-stalker move to lurk this way. He wanted to see Zack. He *needed* to see Zack. To be near him. Talk to him. Touch him. Feel him. Be touched in return. Memories of the last time were branded onto his skin. Zack taking over, taking charge. His hands and mouth all over. Inside.

Just thinking about it made heat rise up to his face and down to his groin.

Zack would make it all better. He'd make the dark memories go away and give him a reason to smile. A reason to be happy about anything.

Brody downed the rest of the whiskey in one gulp and clunked the glass down on the scarred top of the wooden table. He got up, and as he passed the waitress, he did something he'd never done before. Apologized.

"Sorry for being a jackass. Long day." He handed her two twenties to cover the drinks and tip.

"Thanks." She smiled. "I hope your day gets better."

Brody thought about Zack, probably asleep by now. Rumpled bed head and sexy sleep-hooded eyes. "Actually, I think it will."

CHAPTER FOURTEEN

Zack blinked, trying to come awake since there was someone knocking on his door. A well-worn copy of Twain's short stories slid off his chest as he sat up. He rubbed his eyes and looked around. His couch. His home. Had to be late, because he'd worked at the clinic until almost night tonight. Who the freak was knocking at—he checked his watch—midnight?

His heart rate increased. Late-night visitors were rarely good news.

"Hang on!" he yelled through a yawn.

It'd better be Brody, because he'd be the only one visiting at this hour for some reason other than a death in the family or otherwise catastrophic event. Zack padded over to the kitchen in his bare feet and peeked out the glass at the top of the door.

He could tell by the shape and size of the dark silhouette that it was Brody. Brody turned his face to the side, glancing down the street, just enough light to show his expression. Which told Zack exactly nothing, as usual.

"Hey." Zack gave him a smile as he opened the door. "I'm guessing you aren't selling Avon at this hour?"

Brody wrinkled his eyebrows, the joke clearly flying right over his head.

Zack had been raised in an entirely female household. Sometimes he did the mom-joke thing.

"Never mind. Come on in." Zack closed and locked the door behind him. "You okay? I mean, I'm thrilled at a late-night visit from you—don't get me wrong—but usually late hours mean—"

Brody's mouth slammed against his. Zack went right along with it, gripping Brody's arms and tugging him closer. His back hit the mobile island in the kitchen, and it skidded back a foot with the momentum.

"Sorry," Brody muttered, his breath hot and sweet with the scent of whiskey.

"Don't apologize. Do it again."

The slightest smile crossed Brody's lips before they were heavy against Zack's again.

Zack pressed his body against Brody's, tilting his hips so they fit together. And yep, that was Brody's hard-on, already in progress. He had no idea to what he owed the pleasure, but he figured a few whiskey shots played a part. Whatever. It was a hell of a way to wake up, and he wasn't complaining.

"We need to get naked." Brody spoke against his lips.

"Uhm. Okay." Zack grinned. He eased back, allowing just enough room to start on the buttons of Brody's dress shirt as he unhooked the holster. "Are you drunk?" he asked. "Not that it matters. I'll still totally take advantage of you."

The shadow of a smile again from Brody. "I had a few at...Jack's? I think it was called, and walked here. Or was it Mack's?" He tilted his head back to think, and Zack took that moment to lick at the bared neck, forgetting what he'd even asked. "Anyway it was only three in over an hour, so not drunk. I've got a healthy buzz. That's all."

Zack tugged the undershirt up and over Brody's head, flattening his palms against the broad chest. "Well, now I've got a whole different kind of buzz, so thank you, Jack's." He started on Brody's belt, biting back the urge to just grab the hard cock taunting him from behind fabric and start rubbing. No, he wanted flesh on flesh, and part of him kind of wanted buzzed-up Brody to beg for it.

Did that make him the awful tease Brody accused him of being? Probably. And he wasn't even sorry.

He jerked Brody's pants and briefs down in one move, helping him out of his socks and shoes. Then he stood back to have one long, *glorious* look.

"What?" Brody shifted on his feet and took a step toward

him.

"Nothing, I just want a chance to appreciate the view." Fully naked Detective Brody in his kitchen at midnight. Early Merry Christmas to him.

"Enough looking." Brody grabbed him and pulled him toward the hall. He pushed Zack up against one wall, his hot, naked body pressed in so tightly, Zack could feel everything. Somewhere, somehow, he'd done something right in his life. And this was the reward.

Zack pushed back against him, and they fell against the opposite wall, knocking a painting crooked.

"Stay there," Zack said, and stepped back. Away from Brody.

Yeah, he was fucking nuts to do so, but he couldn't resist. Slowly, he pulled his own shirt over his head and let it fall to the floor. One swift tug on his basketball shorts and boxers, and he was just as naked as Brody.

Even in the dimness of the hall, he could see Brody's eyes on him. A storm lit from within, his dark gray gaze hungry with a gleam of danger. It was the first time he'd seen that look so openly from Brody, wanting him, not hiding the fact he'd do anything to catch him.

He reached out without moving closer and ran just his fingertips across the head of Brody's cock, moisture already gathered, coating his fingers before he slid his hand down the underside of the shaft.

Brody moved to touch him too, and Zack smacked his hand away. "Uh-uh. No touching yet. Stand still."

Brody's eyes flashed, and the slightest rumble came from his chest, but Zack knew it was one of approval. As much as Brody was a man of control, there was something within him that liked it when Zack took over. Just so happened, Zack liked it too. *A lot.* He cupped Brody's sac and massaged, stroking his erection with his other hand.

"You want me right now?" he asked.

Brody nodded in a quick, jerky move.

"I want you too. Put your hands on the wall and leave them

there," Zack told him.

A rumble shook Brody's chest. "That's usually my line." But he did exactly that.

Zack moved in, licking and kissing at Brody's throat, stroking his tongue over the Adam's apple and making a hot, wet trail all the way down, stopping to flick his tongue over each nipple until Brody's back arched off the wall.

He knelt in front of Brody and ran both hands up the front of his muscular thighs and down the backs of his legs. He looked up, wanting to see that hunger staring down at him again, wanting to feel the tension in those thick legs, the slightest quiver because he knew Zack could make him come undone.

Brody dipped his chin, his gaze dark, eyes dilated with need.

Zack edged closer, keeping his hands on the backs of Brody's legs. "Don't touch, or I'll stop." With Brody still watching, Zack flicked out his tongue, making the first pass over the head of Brody's cock, then sucking him in, a shudder running up Brody's thighs.

"Fuck...Zack," Brody ground out, still watching him as Zack took him in all the way.

Zack let him slip out of his mouth with a *pop*. "What? You don't like it?" He ran his closed lips across the head again, kissing him there, then ran his tongue underneath, firm licks against the ridge.

Brody's head fell back against the wall with a *thud*, his knees bending slightly. "Yeah," he said, breathing hard as Zack sucked him in and out, in and out. "I just...I..."

Zack watched Brody curl his fingers against the wall, looking for something to hold on to. Needing something to touch.

"I..." Brody inhaled sharply when Zack added his hands, stroking in time with his mouth, every intention of working Brody up enough so he could slide his hand back, slick with desire, and slip his fingers into that tight heat again.

"I... I want you to fuck me," Brody said in a rush.

Zack stopped moving.

He was pretty sure he stopped breathing.

"Wh-what?" He rocked back on his heels to look up at Brody.

Brody still stared at the ceiling. Or, hell, maybe his eyes were closed. He didn't move. Didn't seem to be breathing either.

Zack pushed himself up to stand, because right now, eye contact was a must. "You want me to—"

"You heard me." Brody's gaze finally met his. "Don't act like no one's ever asked you before."

Zack fought the threatening grin, because it really wouldn't be appropriate just yet, even as eagerness thrummed through his body. "Have you ever—"

"No," Brody answered before he could finish.

"You don't even know what I was going to ask."

"Doesn't matter; the answer is still probably no."

Zack felt himself smile a little then. Brave, stoic Brody, still stone-faced and unmoving against the wall in his hall. He stepped in, plied Brody's hands off the wall, and squeezed them. Strong, capable, and surprisingly warm. Just like the man.

Zack knew Brody was so far out of his element here. He was handing something over to Zack, and it probably scared the hell out of him.

Brody didn't look scared, but then, he never would. Solid body, strong shoulders, back rigid, and his face a mask of defined lines and serious angles. He put off an impressive and formidable presence that few could master, but he squeezed Zack's hands in return. Strength and vulnerability. And Zack's heart exploded.

Yup. He was head over heels. Gone. Zack was the fool who let himself get so damn *gone* for this good, dry-witted, but definitely self-protective man. It didn't matter that he would probably get plowed down and stomped on. He would just grin upon impact, because there was no way he'd lift a finger to stop what was already happening. He wanted Brody, and for however long he could have him, he'd hold on.

There were no words, so Zack kissed him. Actually, he had a ton of words, but nothing he was willing to say with the tension sitting on a razor wire. Instead Zack dropped Brody's hands and reached for his face. He brought their lips together and put everything he had into it. He sipped and sucked and stroked at Brody's mouth. Softly, gently, and with every damn emotion swirling in his head.

Finally, Brody relaxed his shoulders. A breathy moan against Zack's lips.

"Okay," he said.

Brody pressed his lips to Zack's, pushing his way inside. He opened, melding their mouths together. Brody tightened his grip on Zack's waist, pulling him closer, the movement rubbing their cocks together with welcome friction. He slid his hands around to the back of Brody's neck, properly plundering his mouth as the kiss grew more urgent with each pass.

Brody pushed off the wall and maneuvered them toward Zack's room. His hands were everywhere, and there was no mistaking the fumbling rush. A desire to hurry and get to the deed itself out of anxiety as much as eagerness.

"Hey," Zack whispered. He pulled back and rained soft kisses along Brody's jaw, the curve of his ear. "There's no rush, okay? In fact...I don't want there to be." He kissed along the muscle of Brody's neck, following to where it met his shoulder. "Just relax."

A nervous laugh from Brody.

Zack straightened, meeting the sharp gray gaze. "You trust me, right?"

"Yeah."

"Then trust I'm going to make it good for you." Good? More like he'd do his best to make it fucking magic. "I...I know you want me to lead, but you've got to let me."

Brody studied his face, his eyes so keen, so clever; Zack felt them go beneath his skin, past bone, seeing right down into his soul. Even as Brody couldn't hide his true desire from Zack, Zack couldn't hide from Brody. The man would know how hard he'd fallen. How imperfect he was despite all the humor and confidence.

And he didn't care.

Let Brody know it all. He was tired of trying to keep him out.

"I will," Brody finally said.

Zack ran his hand to the back of Brody's neck again and dragged him in for a kiss. This time he used the other to reach down, feeling Brody still rock hard against him. He stroked, Brody's breath catching midkiss. He worked him until Brody was completely distracted, breathing through his open mouth, his grip hard on Zack as he let the pleasure build.

"Lie down on the bed," Zack said.

Brody sat down and scooted up enough to straighten his legs. Muscular calves falling to the side as his legs spread slightly, leaning back on his elbows as he watched Zack. It was the hottest thing Zack had ever seen. Certainly the hottest thing ever to be waiting for him like this.

Damn. Going slow was going to be torture.

He grabbed a few things from his nightstand and set them within reach before climbing over Brody. He ran his hands down the breadth of Brody's chest, pausing to brush through the smattering of hair, thumb each nipple. With a quick kiss to Brody's lips, Zack's mouth soon followed his hands. He nibbled at the junction of muscle at Brody's neck, down his sternum, sucking each nipple into his mouth, pressing the flat of his tongue against the nub before continuing down. Each inch of skin skimmed by his hands, muscles gripped and then kissed. When he reached his belly button and placed biting sucks at the strong plane of Brody's stomach, Zack paused in his ministrations and pushed Brody flat onto his back on the bed. A throaty chuckle was the response before he returned to the cut of Brody's hip.

"You're a pushy bastard." Brody sounded warm and thoroughly turned-on but also strained with nerves. That was still too much thinking in Zack's book, so he ran one hand down a strong quad and then up, brushing the soft skin of his inner thigh and skimming so close to Brody's sac that Brody groaned in frustration.

Zack looked up to catch Brody's gaze and grinned. Brody's eyes were liquid heat as he wet his lips. "And a fucking tease."

He grinned again and moved his hand to encircle the erection that was too damn gorgeous to ignore any longer. "This is news?" Zack stroked once, twice, and then caught the head, thumbing the moisture.

Brody's mouth opening with a heated breath was exactly the look he was going for. "You're a detective or something, right? That's how you caught on?"

Brody chuckled, the sound deep and rolling. His eyes crinkled at the corners, wet mouth tugging up crookedly.

It was the most undone and free Zack had ever seen him. Nothing short of beautiful.

Something must have shown on Zack's face. Not that it was a surprise. He knew all he felt for Brody, the way he had fallen so hard and so deep, was probably there blinking in bright yellow lights over his head. He didn't want to freak Brody out with a bunch of feelings, but there was no stopping it.

Brody didn't freak out, at least not that Zack could tell. He didn't freeze, tense up, or pull the mask back on. Instead he reached down and brushed Zack's hair out of his face and cupped his cheek, thumb brushing over his lips, sliding over the wetness.

"I remember the first time I saw you," Brody said. "You ran in late for my PT appointment. I can see it in my mind like it's a damn snapshot. Your hair all in your face from rushing, but the whole professional-therapist thing pulled around you like a Kevlar vest. You were so fucking hot—*are*—so fucking hot," he added when Zack tilted his head. "I wasn't just pissed about my bum knee and the pain. I was pissed because I was thinking, *This* is who will be all up in my space, rehabbing me? Who'd I piss off to have to endure this hell? This is never going to work. Fucking look at him.'"

Zack laughed, still stroking Brody's thighs, using the back of his hand to brush over Brody's sac, his thick cock. "Yeah. And look at me now."

This time Brody's laugh was full, nothing held back. It shook his chest and the whole damn bed.

God, he loved that sound. "I remember you too," Zack said. "Back when I never saw you laugh or even knew you were capable. No matter how ridiculously hot you were, I knew you were going to be difficult. I thought you were going to be a complete tool."

Brody still laughed. "I am a complete tool."

Zack slid his hands up Brody's sides so he flinched from the tickling sensation. "Yeah, but now I know you, so it's okay. You're my tool."

As soon as he said it, he wanted to swallow his tongue. He shouldn't presume that Brody was okay with being his anything. But hell, he'd asked Zack to be his first. That meant something, no matter how much it probably proved Zack was a sap.

Brody gave him a barely there smile, eyes warming as he caressed Zack's arm and moved over to his own cock, stroking it before Zack stopped him.

"Nice try," he said, and replaced it with his own touch, wrapping his hand around the thick base of Brody's cock before flicking his tongue over the head and taking it into his mouth. He found the right pace, Brody arching and flexing his lower back with each suck, obviously holding back the urge to fuck Zack's mouth. Instead Zack swallowed him down, Brody's cock hitting the back of his throat. Brody gripped the sheets in response, head thrown back.

"Oh...yeah," he ground out.

Zack moved down, dragging his tongue across Brody's sac before sucking each ball into his mouth, one at a time. Then he began again at the top. He kept going until Brody was a lust-hazed, writhing mess.

"Fuck," Brody said, voice strained.

Zack sat up. "Roll over," he told Brody.

There was no hesitation. Brody turned over onto his stomach, tucking his hands under Zack's pillow.

Holy hell, that pillow was going to smell of Brody now. His shampoo and aftershave and own individual scent. And Zack was absolutely the guy who'd face-plant into it later and take a whiff, seeing exactly this: the glorious sight before him. Brody facedown, muscled legs spread wide, perfectly round ass angled up. Wanting and waiting for Zack. It was all he could do not to grab his own dick and jerk off at the view.

He moved over Brody, massaging each cheek, still convinced that both should be illegal.

"Come up on your knees a little," Zack told him, and grabbed a spare pillow to slide underneath. Reaching under, he used Brody's precum and the moisture from his mouth to massage the sensitive area between his balls and his ass. Brody wriggled and squirmed at the sensation, until Zack found the right spot and pressure.

When Brody pressed back against his touch, the movement pushing his ass in the air just so, Zack flicked his tongue over Brody's opening. The ragged breathing near the head of the bed was all the encouragement he needed. He kept going. The taunting flicks giving way to the slightest pressure. Swirling strokes as he kneaded Brody's ass.

"Zack...fuck...*Zack*." The quiet, pleading praise started again, just like in the shower, and Zack was certain he'd never hear his name sound as sensual.

He grabbed the small bottle of lube and coated his fingers.

"Brody," he said, settling onto his knees, brushing his thumb over Brody's opening, grinning at the moan it caused. "You like that, don't you?" he asked, and did it again. He alternated between barely a caress and massaging with the slightest pressure in. Yes, he was teasing Brody, and yes, he knew Brody fucking loved it.

Brody didn't respond with words. He moved on the bed, hands digging into the spread, strong thighs shifting to push his ass toward Zack's touch. Zack watched the ripple of his quad muscles, the way he pressed his face into the mattress. A low groan came out muffled when Zack slowly dipped the tip of his finger in, pushing on the rim. He knew how that felt, how intense it was to be fingered so slowly. The torture of it as those muscles both fought and ached for it.

He wanted that for Brody.

Another slow circle around the rim, and Zack pressed the tip of a finger in to the second knuckle. "You're so gorgeous like this, Brody." He pulled out slowly, circling and gathering lube before entering the warmth again. Faster this time. Making it feel like fucking. "I've pictured you so many times. Pictured this ass in so many different ways." Slow out, fast in. "*God*, I can't wait to fuck you."

Brody's breath caught on an inhale, his back arching lower. He reached back as if to touch Zack's hand. "Mmmm more," he murmured.

Zack squeezed Brody's cheek with his other hand, tempering himself. The view was enough to cause him to blow completely. Add to that, Brody's new discovery of extreme pleasure was because of Zack's fingers. Zack being in him. Damn, he needed a gazillion Valium and a long meditation retreat to calm down.

Instead he took a few breaths to compose and gave Brody the *more* he'd asked for. As if he could deny Brody anything. Zack slicked the second finger, pushing both in and letting a third press against the rim. "Breathe for me, Brody. Breathe and push back against me."

Brody did exactly as Zack asked. He was stretched tight around Zack's fingers, and it sent a bolt of pure want. *Need.*

"*Damn.*" Zack swore. He wanted to feel that around him, like yesterday. But this was a huge undertaking, being the first one inside Brody. He *was* going slowly.

He pushed his fingers in, moving and curling them just right. He knew he'd found what he'd been looking for when Brody nearly arched off the bed. Zack grinned as he pulled back to thrust in again, but before he could, a hand locked on to his thigh. Brody's strong hand clamping down and squeezing. He had turned his head and was now looking up at Zack. Eyes hazy, mouth open and panting.

"Damn it, Zack." His voice was raw, and he paused to lick his lips. "If you don't get *in* me now, I know a lot of dangerous people. I can be one of them."

It made Zack laugh, smile pulling at his face so hard it ached. "I love it when you get all bad cop." He pulled his fingers out and reached for the condom, ripping the foil. He had to close his eyes as he rolled it on. The pressure and the application of additional lube *while* staring at Brody's ass would make for an unremarkably quick ending. He bit off a groan and squeezed the base of his dick.

"Okay." Zack slid up, steadying himself between Brody's legs with a hand on his hip. "Just like before, breathe out, and push against me." Zack lined himself up, gripping Brody tight as he pressed slowly, waiting for the give.

As the tip gave way and squeezed at Zack's head, Brody turned his face to the pillow again and groaned into it. Zack could totally understand the sentiment. He took another breath and waited.

Seemed Brody didn't want to wait. His strong hand was back, and he grabbed at Zack's thigh, urging him forward and in. The tightness and heat were so overwhelming that Zack gasped loudly, his body falling over Brody's from the force. He pressed his face into the broad back and tried to breathe.

"Holy hell, Brody." Zack's voice almost didn't come back to him; it came out thready and tight. "Not wise to kill me now; I haven't even started." He kissed the smooth skin. Brody's back moved up and down, his breathing hard.

Brody angled his head the best he could and moved his hands up to tug at Zack wrist. "Come here."

Zack leaned over to kiss messily at the side of Brody's mouth. It was off-center and awkward, but Brody groaned against his mouth because leaning over caused Zack to thrust fully in, hard.

"All right." Brody panted. "Now...fuck me." He gave Zack's thigh one last reassuring squeeze and turned his head, pressing his ass fully against Zack. And there was no arguing with that.

Zack settled his hands along Brody's waist, pressing one last kiss to his back as he eased back and slowly pushed in. The tight heat. The feel of Brody's powerful body pressed full against him. Zack *had* to go slowly; each thrust felt like it would be the last. He dug his hands into the sheets and focused on the movement. He experimented with angle, finding his place inside. It'd been a while since he'd taken the time not to just fuck someone but please them, and Brody wasn't just someone. Zack loved him.

Yup. Zack had fallen in love with Brody. Completely and stupidly. The best kind. The kind that made you want to torture yourself with slow sex just so you could find that rhythm that made your partner go—

"Oh *God!*" Brody bucked forward, hands grabbing new fistfuls of sheets before shoving his ass right back toward Zack. "Fuck, yes! That! Zack..." He made it sound like a warning if Zack didn't repeat immediately.

Zack thrust in again, getting the same response. Each slide into Brody, Zack hit hard and on point. Each time he drew back, he felt his head spin. By the fifth time, Brody completely lost it.

"God *dammit.*" Brody reached out, clutching at anything, and grabbed the rest of the pillows, digging his hands into the plush, his swearing muffled but very dirty.

Brody's back heaved, and Zack had to close his eyes again to focus. To make it last.

"*Fuck. Me.* Zack…harder." Brody tried to move, but Zack grabbed on to hold him. No way was he losing this angle now.

He cursed against Brody's sweaty skin. "It's okay. I got you."

"Fuck." The word was muffled but on repeat as Brody shifted, trying to move his hand underneath him. His body started shaking as he jacked himself off. "Zack… *Please.*"

And that was it. There was no way Zack could hold back any longer. He settled his weight further and fucked him with harder and quicker thrusts, catapulting them both toward the end.

Brody made pleading, grunting noises as Zack pushed him farther, urged him on. "Come on, Brody. Come for me. I want to feel you feel you come while you're wrapped around me."

Brody let out a strangled cry and shuddered, long and hard, his body tightening as he came. He grabbed back at Zack again, digging his fingers into the muscle of his leg and bringing Zack closer, deeper.

Finally, Zack let himself go, hips pistoning fast and irregular as he followed Brody over the crest of that wave. He came with his fingers gripping Brody's hips so hard there was no way it wouldn't bruise.

They lay there panting. Zack gave up on holding himself off Brody and face-planted into his sweaty back, the thrum of Brody's heart against his face. With barely enough energy, Zack groaned as he slowly withdrew, pulling off the condom and letting it drop onto the floor.

"*Fuck,*" Brody finally said, falling forward and slowly

turning his head to the side.

"Yeah." Zack tried to catch his breath.

With a moan, Brody pressed back and pushed Zack to the side and off of him.

Zack couldn't even protest. He just rolled over, closed his eyes, and tried to catch his breath. "*Wow.*"

"Yeah," Brody agreed.

What else could they say? Zack had certainly had some amazingly athletic sex in his life, but nothing had left him as blissful and worn as this.

Zack felt the bed move and the heat of Brody's body. He opened his eyes to find Brody looking down at him. Flushed, face and lips red, breathing heavy. And smiling.

If the sex didn't kill him, Brody's smile—

Brody kissed him. Cupped the side of his face, leaned down, and kissed him. That deep, soul-destroying kind of kiss that was gentle and caring and dirty as hell. Tongues sliding in to taste, lips pulling, sucking. His hands were soft, fingers moving to brush through Zack's hair. It felt exactly as Zack bet it was meant to. It told him all he needed to know and what he knew it'd take forever to actually say.

Brody was gone on him too. He'd fallen just as hard.

CHAPTER FIFTEEN

The bed moved beneath Brody, dipping with the weight of something heavy. Something heavy...and moose-like.

He grinned into the pillow at the thought and turned his head. The morning sunlight was bright and unforgiving as it poured into Zack's room. But somehow Zack still managed to look like the cover of a men's fitness magazine, perfect smile and all.

"Morning, sunshine. Coffee?" Zack grinned, one knee on the bed, holding two of the biggest coffee mugs known to man, both emblazoned with armadillos in cowboy outfits.

Brody pushed up to one elbow and squinted at the mugs. "You aren't right in the head...but thanks."

Zack passed one over and sat next to him. "Don't give my armadillos the stink eye. I'll gladly take that mug back if you're going to insult it."

"I'd never insult cowboy armadillos," Brody lied.

"These are the biggest mugs they had at South of the Border."

He managed to sit up without spilling any of the vital nectar and leaned back against the headboard. "You actually went *into* South of the Border? Why? It's a tacky-ass tourist trap for Yankees."

"Because, it's a tacky-ass tourist trap and it's awesome. Where else can you find cowboy armadillo coffee mugs along with some sweet flip-flop salt-and-pepper shakers?" Zack grinned even bigger and maneuvered his way up next to Brody. His teeth were bright in his tan face, relaxed joy pouring off him like the sun into his room.

Zack was in a good mood nine times out of ten, but this was a shit-eating-grin-type good mood. He beamed, and the possibility that it was because of Brody was...

He shook it off. There was no fucking way. He'd never made anyone happy, never mind *this* happy. The kind of happiness that made other people jealous and a little bit nauseated.

Zack leaned over, coffee balanced in one hand, and kissed Brody full on the lips with the sweet taste of cinnamon creamer. "To say last night was...wow is an understatement, because I can't come up with great words until I've had another coffee." He leaned back. "But I know it was new. Y'know...for you, and I'm glad it was... I'm glad I was the one who...was with you when—"

"You love that you were my first. Just spit it out." Brody sipped his coffee.

Zack smirked. "Okay. I'm glad I was your first and that it was...y'know?"

Brody raised his eyebrows, still sipping.

"Y'know..."

"Awesome?"

Zack sighed and rolled his eyes. "Yes, it was awesome. For me too. I mean, that's not the norm."

Brody didn't respond right away, his mind thrown back to last night. Awesome didn't begin to describe it. He'd imagined letting go, letting someone take over, take control, and do that to him, *for* him, for years. But he felt vulnerable even thinking about it, and he wasn't about to be vulnerable with anyone.

Except Zack.

To finally be with someone, not only someone he cared about, but who so obviously cared about him in return, and for it to surpass "awesome" was what he didn't expect in his life. He'd spent years accepting that this was something he'd never have. Yet here he was.

Zack shifted on the bed. "I mean, I'm just saying—" A note of anxiety laced through his voice in response to Brody's silence.

Brody shook his head as he set down his enormous coffee mug. He leaned over and took Zack's face in both hands, kissing him again so he'd shut the fuck up. He sucked at Zack's lips, teasing him with flicks of his tongue, until he pulled a groan from Zack.

"It was better than awesome. I know amazing sex when I've had it," Brody said. "Even if I haven't let myself have any before. And no, I'm not freaked out about finally letting you top me. I've thought about it a lot. A hell of a lot since I met you."

"Oh yeah?" Zack failed at containing his grin.

Brody elbowed Zack's coffee-free arm. "It was intense, better than I'd imagined...and I fucking loved it—if that wasn't obvious enough for you last night, I'm telling you now. So don't worry. I'm as sold on you as you are on me."

Zack blinked at him, brown eyes so big and dark they were like looking out at the sea at night.

"Relax and drink your coffee, okay?"

"Okay."

"There is one problem," Brody said before sitting back and taking a long sip of his coffee. It was an asshole thing to do, but Zack wasn't the only one who could be an awful tease.

"What?" Zack shifted to look at him. "What is it?"

"I'm starving. I want some pizza from that Woodchuck's place again. And you're buying."

They spent the rest of the morning doing a whole lot of nothing and eventually wandered down Center Street in Folly Beach to the hole-in-the-wall surfer bar and pizza shop.

"Best pizzas ever. I told you," Zack announced.

He wasn't lying either. They ordered two large supremes, one for each of them, and waddled home with only four leftover slices.

"Just go on without me." Zack stopped halfway back to his house and leaned against a palmetto tree, holding his nonexistent belly. "I...I'm too full. I..." He staggered. "I can't go on. Save yourself."

Brody laughed, remembering the last time Zack made the same joke. They'd known each other over two months now. In a way, they'd been together for over two months. Two months. The realization was startling, but in a good way.

"No!" Brody said, playing along this time. "I won't leave you here. Mainly because you're the one carrying the leftover pizza, and I may want some later." He grabbed Zack's free arm and threw it across his shoulder.

"All for one and one trying to rob the last of my pizza," Zack proclaimed with a fist in the air.

Brody laughed, not thinking about who might see them acting like fools. "Don't make me laugh." He groaned. "I'm too full to laugh."

"You and me both," Zack agreed. "Carry me." He tried flinging a moose-long leg up into Brody's arm.

"Hell no." Brody swatted his leg away. "I'll go get your wheelbarrow and haul you back before I carry your big ass."

"Ha! Like you could haul me anywhere."

Brody straightened, shaking off Zack's arm. "Is that a challenge?"

"Oh." Zack nodded with the adamancy of a district court judge. "Oh that's a challenge."

"Fine. Stay right there." He started walking away but thought better about it. He spun around, grabbed the pizza box, and then headed toward Zack's.

"Hey!" Zack called after him but didn't move from his spot on the side of the road. "Pizza thief! Someone stop him! I'm calling the cops! Oh, wait."

Brody laughed or grinned the three blocks back to Zack's. Even after devouring the majority of an enormous pizza, he felt...light. The heaviness of the job, his case, having to max his upcoming PT test, it was all momentarily lifted. Paused. Compartmentalized. He was having fun. *Fun.*

What the fuck?

He found the wheelbarrow in the lean-to shed next to the sailboat, and Zack started cackling as soon as he rolled up.

"Holy shit!" Zack laughed. "You win. I never imagined it possible, but you have beaten me at shenanigans. Oh, *and* it's like makeshift PT. We are brilliant. Best day ever." He eased back in the wheelbarrow, long legs hanging over the sides, fingers locked behind his head as Brody laid the pizza box on his lap. "Let's go home, but if you try to dump me out on the side of the road, then it's forty pushups for you." He nodded forward, and Brody began pushing him, knowing he wore the same stupid grin as Zack.

CHAPTER SIXTEEN

When Brody finished his two-mile qualifying run, he knew. He'd killed it. Kicked that PT exam's ass.

He walked it out, his body on fire and alive with the effort of the competency testing. His marksmanship the day before had been better than when he was in the damn academy. Clocked a level twelve on the beep test, flying beyond the pass level of ten with a mental *Fuck yeah!*

He'd be back on Homicide and finishing the case before week's end. Zack was a man of his word. He'd not only gotten Brody up to code, he'd helped him kick its ass. But then, Zack being a man of his word had never been in question.

The last night spent with him had been... Brody cleared his throat. Even the memories made him both hotter than the two-mile run and warmer than the summer breeze. Their day together after had been relaxed. Natural. Happy.

Zack was constant in his personality, his promises, and his desires. The man was a giant spaz with a few anxiety issues, but he knew who he was and what he wanted. He'd made it clear he wanted Brody.

Why? Brody hadn't a fucking clue. Zack deserved better. A hell of a lot better than what he could ever offer.

"Damn, Brody!" The tester approached him as he came back around the track and handed him water. "Nice time. You doing growth hormone or some shit? Aren't you knocking on forty or something? What's the secret?"

"I'm thirty-three, asshole. You know that. We graduated

academy together."

The guy laughed and smacked him on the back. "For real, nice going. It'll be good to have you back on the job soon."

Those were the words ringing through his head when he met with his captain the next day. Back on the job. Soon. So fucking soon.

It wouldn't be soon enough.

He and Lamont had a job to do, and with what they'd discussed about the Strangler, he knew if he could get both their eyes on this latest case, they'd close it. His gut was never wrong, and there was something they were missing. They'd find it, he had no doubt. They'd find it and nail the sonuvabitch terrorizing their city.

"Brody." Captain Hill grabbed his hand in a firm shake. "It's damn good to know you're going to be off desk duty and back out there."

"It's damn good to be going back." Brody sat as his captain circled the desk, taking his seat.

"I'm sure you can guess I've kept in touch with Lamont, Officer Davis, and I feel confident we can hit our caseload like we never missed a day."

Hill's eyebrows pinched as he scooted forward and grabbed the manila file on his desk. "I'm sure you could." He chuckled, and it was forced, false noise.

The sound of it turned Brody's stomach.

"But if you've been in touch with Lamont, you know he's partners with Griggs now." Hill centered the file on his desk pad and tapped a pen against it. "They're doing a good job and finally have some viable leads with the Strangler. I'm putting you in Robbery. Captain O'Connor will be your new CO. They need someone like you to—"

"You've got to be shitting me," Brody interrupted his captain as the floor seemed to tilt beneath him.

"Excuse me?"

Brody gave him the same false laugh in return. "Very funny, now be serious. Me on Robbery and Lamont with Griggs is the worst fucking idea ever, so I know you've got to be kidding."

Hill shook his head, lowering his gaze to the file. "I wish I was kidding. But you didn't hear that from me. You're on Robbery, Brody. Griggs stays."

"You can't look me in the eye and say it, because you know it's bullshit."

"It is what it is." He looked up and narrowed his eyes at Brody. "Accept it. I've had to."

"I get it." Realization dawned. "This wouldn't have anything to do with Griggs being the chief's favorite nephew-in-law or whatever, now would it? He's connected, so I get screwed?"

Hill shrugged.

"Son of a bitch." He chewed on the words. He could argue until he lost his voice; it wouldn't make any difference. "At least keep me on Homicide, Captain. Eventually Griggs is going to screw up bad enough to get tossed to the side. Come on."

"I wish I could. I've got no slots. Budget is tapped out on staff as it is. I'm stuck."

"You're stuck?"

"You think I want to lose you to Robbery? *Robbery?* Hell no! But I'm friends with O'Connor, and I know when something opens up here, he'll make it a simple transfer for me to get you back."

"This is bureaucratic bullshit, and you know it."

"Your career at the department won't suffer. You'll be back in Homicide as soon as—"

"Screw my career. What about my case? That's my case, and you think Griggs is going to solve it? Another girl will die."

"Hey!" Hill slapped his hand against the file. "I won't let that happen. I'm doing all I can about your position too, so don't chew my ass for trying to help. I could just say fuck you and off you go."

Brody chewed on the inside of his lip. He knew that was true, but it did nothing to ease the sucker punch of being officially tossed off his case.

"I knew it," he said, his voice heating up. "I knew this shit was going to happen. And you know Griggs will never solve this case. That's what this is all about, some glory whore who wants his name in the paper for collaring the decade's bad guy, and he's going to fuck it up. You and I both know it."

Captain Hill sat expressionless.

"More deaths because he's a well-connected, entitled tool bag who can't do the job, and I happened to trick up my knee."

Still not even a blink of a reaction. Hill just slid the file across the desk toward him. "Your new assignment. You start tomorrow. I'll bring you back on as soon as I can."

Brody stared at the manila cover but only saw the last victim's face. Her photo from the track-and-field sports club. So much promise. So much life. He was tired of seeing their faces.

He snatched the file up without a word. He wanted to storm from the office, slam the door back against the wall, but he wouldn't give Griggs the satisfaction. Just in case the fucker was somewhere nearby.

Instead he walked out without a word, not even a heavy footfall. When he got home, he put his fist through the wall.

An hour later, his phone rang.

He answered it without looking, expecting it to be Zack.

"I just got your message. Mother*fuck*!"

"Hey, Lamont." Brody stretched his fingers wide and replaced the ice pack, knuckles still singing.

"How come you don't sound pissed? I chew Hill a new one...then he chews me one for disrespect, and you don't even sound bothered."

"You fucking kidding me? I did the same thing. Now I'm worn out from the adrenaline rush, staring at this new hole in my wall, and thinking maybe I need to calm my ass down."

Silence on the other end, then, "I wanted to punch one too, but Felicia would kill me."

"Where are you now?"

"On my way over, but I swear to God, man, you didn't get these from me. You took them yourself; you don't even know my damn name. We understand?"

"It's our fucking case, Lamont. And a few copies of the latest case notes aren't going to get you sacked. I would take all the files—originals—if I knew it'd get the job done."

"All right, all right. I said I'm bringing them over, didn't I? You still have copies of your old notes?"

"I got them." Of course he did. And Lamont knew it. Brody had never let this case go cold.

—✦—

Brody glanced over at the drawn blinds, the sun forcing its way through the sides. It had to be midday at least. He shifted his focus to the blank wall beside the window, anything far away and easy on the eyes, because they were fucking killing him from staring at small print on white pages all night until he passed out.

"Shit." He rubbed each lid with a forefinger. Not only had he been demoted and kicked off his case, he had a reading-and-whiskey hangover and would probably need glasses sometime in the next ten years, and that just pissed him off.

He sat up and put his feet on the floor, his head pounding in protest. Coffee.

Coffee was what he needed. He'd had just this side of too much last night, but he knew he wouldn't have slept without it.

"Shit." Brody tripped over his copy of the most recent Strangler file that Lamont smuggled over.

He made his way to the coffeepot, and by the time he'd had a piss and washed his hands and face, there was a full pot waiting on him. Beckoning with promises of a clear head and finally being able to see what he hadn't seen in the last ten fucking years. The old files he practically had memorized, and in the new one, there was nothing that jumped out as any different other than the time between.

There was something vital there, and he wasn't seeing it.

That was the only explanation for why this case remained unsolved. There he was, throwing stones at Griggs, when his sorry ass couldn't get the job done either.

"*Fuck.*" He sighed.

If he had to study the files until his eyes fell out of his head in order to solve it, then that was what he'd do. He couldn't work the case actively anymore, but he could fix this. He could bring these girls justice and hopefully save a few more.

He'd study this thing and figure out what they were *all* missing.

He was two sips into his second cup of coffee when there was a loud thumping on his front door.

"Hey! Brody. You alive?"

Zack.

Brody got up from his small kitchen table, hands going to his hair so at least he wouldn't look like complete shit upon answering the door.

He opened it to find Zack in his work polo and slacks. There was none of that now-familiar grin, just concern pinching his eyebrows.

"Hey." Brody kept it casual.

"Don't 'hey' me." Zack wasn't having it. "You disappear completely for two straight days—no call, no text, no reply when *I* call and text to ask how you did on your PT, no jack shit. I know you were getting news about your job, and you want to give me a *hey?*"

Brody backed up to let him in. "I didn't disappear. I'm right here. I've just been...busy."

Zack stopped just inside the door, the pinched look still on his face. "Busy? Normally, I get a reply within a couple of hours, definitely before forty-eight, so don't act like I'm being all"—he waved his fingers in the air—"needy or paranoid. Two days go by, and I don't hear shit? I'm wondering if you're back on active, if you got hurt, or worse, given your line of work..."

He let the sentence go, then shrugged and studied some point beyond Brody's left shoulder.

The vulnerability in that look made Brody realize he was being an asshole. Old habits died hard. All Zack had ever done was help him get back in shape, and it was natural to worry when your...your...whatever the fuck they were...when one of you was a homicide detective.

Except Brody wasn't a homicide detective. Not anymore.

"Yeah, I— Sorry. It's been..." He didn't want to go into what it'd been. Zack didn't need to know the darkness of some of his corners. "Come on in. Ignore the mess." He led the way past the kitchen and dining area. "You want some coffee?" He grabbed his cup as Zack followed him to the den.

"No, I'm...good?"

Brody glanced back to see his gaze lingering over the coffee table, the mess of folders and papers, whiskey bottle.

"Sorry." Brody closed each file and stacked it all up as neatly as possible. There was nothing there Zack should see.

He grabbed the whiskey bottle and returned it to the kitchen, opening the blinds on the way back.

"I'm going to guess this is about work," Zack said as he sat down next to him. "Because you're walking just fine, and you aren't pissed off at me, that I'm aware of."

"Yeah." Brody nodded. He didn't want to talk to Zack about work or the case or any of the shit from the last two days, but he did deserve some type of explanation.

"Your place has a kind of... It has a very angry bear-cave feel to it, and you look a little rough." He turned and touched Brody's day-and-a-half-old stubble. "This I like, though," he commented before pressing his lips to Brody's.

Brody let himself fall into the kiss for just a moment, lips closed, a few seconds' reprieve from real life's shit pile, before pulling away.

"Okay." Zack sighed and beckoned with his hand. "What's going on? You never pull away, so talk to me. Feel free to leave out any gory details, but say something, because seriously? You look and feel like you're ready to snap. No offense."

He knew he looked like hell, and Zack would only badger him until he came out with it, but he'd only ever talked to Zack about work a couple of times. Both times it was about old, long-closed cases, and both times he still hadn't wanted to talk about it. Just did it because there was no avoiding it.

This was different. This case was current and a part of him. His shadow. It was woven into who he was, and for reasons he couldn't grasp, it didn't feel natural to open up to Zack about it. It was like worlds fucking colliding, and it was two worlds that he never mixed. Worlds he'd never intended to mix. His giving lover and his job as a homicide detective.

No!

He didn't want to talk to anyone about work, especially not Zack. He wanted to sit, alone, with his files and think. Be pissed at the world and find the bastard who had taken another life from this world like it was his fucking right.

None of it had anything to do with Zack—and that was how Brody preferred it. He couldn't think about Zack while he was thinking about his job or vice versa. Force of habit, and he didn't function that way. Work meant only work. Not family, not friends, not anything.

Zack wouldn't get it. He wouldn't understand what the job meant, because they met during the freak-accident part of Brody's life. The anomaly of Brody having free time, not working his ass off as a detective, not being married to the job.

Zack's sun-warmed face pinched further as he shifted on the couch again, the tension in his shoulders evident. "Well?"

There would be no deflecting or dodging what was going on. Brody wouldn't even try.

"I've been asked to back off on a case. *The* case. The one I've been involved in since I was a probie." Brody didn't know what else to say. How did he express all the nights this case had haunted him? How his job was all he'd ever had. It was his life.

Understanding widened Zack's eyes for a moment. "But you passed your PT, right?"

"I killed it." Brody nodded, staring at his hands, the hangnail on his right index finger. "Thanks to you."

"So why wouldn't they put you back to full duty?"

"I am. But this case was being worked on while I was on leave and light, and the captain doesn't want a high-profile case to be passing around to too many hands. There was another murder while I was gone, so…"Brody tightened his hands at that thought, because he refused to let go. "I get screwed over. And I'm pretty sure there's a lot of bullshit politics at play here too. Now I'm not even in homicide. I'm working robbery."

His voice was sharpening. Yet another reason he did not want to talk about this with Zack. He felt sharp. The momentum of reading over the case files was the only thing that smoothed him out. Zack wanting to talk about it? Not really helping. He was in cop mode, and cope mode wasn't one that'd blend well with being-around-Zack mode.

"Y'know..." Brody scrubbed a hand through his hair. "I...we don't have to talk about my work anymore. Really," Brody tried. "I'd rather not."

"You can't help with the case anyway?" Zack pushed.

Brody glanced over and found Zack's expression totally in earnest. He leaned his elbows on his knees and waited for Brody's response. That was Zack. Open. Patient. Such a decent guy. The kind of guy who deserved everything. All the things Brody would never be able to give him.

He felt a low tug in his gut that reminded him who was the one lacking in this equation.

"This is the second warning for me to stay off the case. Really, man, I don't want to—"

"Whoa. What do you mean second warning?" Zack sat forward a little.

The tension in Brody's chest rose again, causing an ache that made it hard to breathe. "As in, I've already been told, indirectly, not to be involved. Now I've been told again, officially, to fuck off."

"I don't—" Zack touched his forehead as if to stop the flow of words. "I mean when? When did all this happen? I've known you for months now, and I didn't know all of this was going on with your job. I thought things were okay. I'm here without a clue about what's going on in your life?"

It started to build again inside of Brody. The frustration that he'd ignored for the last day. The same resentment and anger that ended with his fist in the wall. "When I was on paid leave, my partner still had this case. I went to a scene, was reminded it was not my scene. When I aced my PT because I worked...*we* worked to make it happen, I was told to stay off this case. I'm still not listening, so I'm sure I'll be told again to fuck off when they should let me do my job."

"I...I don't understand."

"Yeah. I know." That edge in his voice was getting brusque. He could hear what he didn't say. *You'll never understand, so I'm going to sound condescending no matter what. May as well not bother trying not to.* "They don't want me to help, because I'm not even in the same fucking department anymore. Normally a cop's case is his case, but oh no. I've been moved to Robbery and cut off. Do I look like a Robbery guy to you? So I say fuck them and their orders. I'm working this case anyway. I don't care if they suspend me; this has to stop."

Zack's eyes went wide. "Is it wise to just say fuck them?"

Brody shot to his feet. "You're taking their side?"

"No." Zack held his hands up, a conceding gesture. "Jeez, you should know I'm on your side. I'm just trying to grasp what you're saying."

Brody started pacing, the room shrinking around him. It was too damn hot in his den now. And stuffy. He jerked open the glass door by the kitchen table.

"Why didn't you tell me any of this before?" Zack asked. "Why avoid me for days?"

Good question, but Zack wouldn't like the answer. "Because I just didn't want to get into it. Not with everything else going on. I don't want to be discussing it now, yet here we are."

There was long, tight silence until Brody finally looked over at Zack.

"Okay," Zack said, the muscles in his neck and jaw working. "So they give you what you consider a downgraded job, cause this huge change in your life that clearly upsets you, and you don't want to talk about it? At all?"

Zack's gaze burned through Brody as he nodded.

"Is that why I get the feeling you're mad at me?" Zack managed. "I'm just trying to help you."

"By giving me the third degree? All while sitting there, righteously pissed at me for trying to deal with this in my way and not drag you into my shit pile? This is my issue. Not yours. I'm saving you from this, and I told you at least three times I *didn't* want to talk about it, but here we are. Talking about it."

ZACK TOOK A breath and tried not to let the sheer anger rolling off Brody knock him off the couch. But his words still hit like a fist to the chest. He'd been on the receiving end of another man's unhappiness before. Felt the blame through harsh words and icy-cold withdrawal, when the fault was far from ever being Zack's.

And third degree? Righteous? What the hell? He got that this case meant a great deal, but Brody was shutting him out and expecting him not to be offended. And then being a shithead about it.

Being shut out was not going to happen. Zack was pretty sure they'd passed that option a couple of fucks ago.

He tried to keep his voice level. "I'm helping by being here for you when you've completely ignored me even though you need someone to talk to." Okay, he'd done it. He'd tried. Now breathe. Be supportive. "Brody. I get it. It sucks."

Brody gave him a look like razor blades might fly forth from his eyes. His thick arms were still crossed.

"Okay. It *really* sucks. But I'm not the bad guy here. I'm trying, even if failing, to help." Zack ran a hand through his hair as Brody took up his pacing again.

He felt like he was outside a thick piece of glass, looking in. Watching Brody, seeing him run headlong into disaster but unable to get through or make him stop and see. He *hated* that feeling, and he hated being helpless as Brody reverted back into someone he hardly knew. "So what are you going to do?"

"What do you think I'm going to do? Keep working on it." Brody walked over to the chair next to the couch and grabbed a file like he was going to do exactly that. Right now. "Griggs thinks he's all over this. Kid is an idiot and a royal prick to boot. I'll have this figured out while he just sits with his thumb up his ass. I've got a few ideas. He's got jack."

"Do you think that's a good idea?" he tried to ask again as delicately as possible. Brody wanted nothing to do with discussing the matter, but Zack loved the guy. There was no denying that anymore. And there was no way he'd sit here and let Brody shoot himself in the foot.

Brody looked up at him, his expression hard. Zack didn't like that look on him at all. He hadn't seen it in weeks, and now he remembered how much he hated it.

"*I* get to make that call. And yes, I absolutely think this is a good idea. Furthermore, I think that if I don't work this case, there'll be another dead girl in a few weeks and still no leads and that'll be on me. You think you could handle that with a smile?" He turned back to the folders on the table, hands balled into fists, knuckles white against the sea of manila and brown folders.

Zack couldn't stand it anymore. He got up and walked over to Brody. His broad shoulders didn't relax an inch. "I know it's important," Zack told him. "The most important, and it's also your job." He placed a hand gently on Brody's shoulder. The muscles were tense, like a coiled spring. "So what happens at the third warning? Your job is everything to you, but I don't think you should push it, and I definitely don't want you getting hurt. You really want to risk that?"

Brody turned to look up at him. The action shrugged Zack's hand away. "*I* get to make that call. Not you."

Zack opened his mouth to say something but was cut off with a point of Brody's finger. "You're not my mother. You're not my wife. You don't have a say in this."

The floor fell from beneath Zack, and the dropping sensation was way too familiar. Way too real. He was launched back to college and every year since he'd accepted his sexuality. Too many parties, too few real relationships. The heart-crushing awareness of being the closeted guy's dirty little secret. He was tossed back into childhood, being in the way, a burden rather than beloved. He knew this feeling too well. Being a hindrance, a problem...of being worth nothing.

He blinked at Brody, no idea if he was waiting for a smirk, a break in the concrete facade, a quick apology or plea to let him take it back. He was waiting for something. Something to dispel the pain of what Brody had just said.

It never came.

Brody remained expressionless except for the anger pulling at the corners of his eyes. The silence drew out as he turned back to his files like he was dismissing Zack. For life, for all he knew. Regardless, it was a clear dismissal.

Zack took a deep breath and counted to ten. He knew a snake about to strike when he saw one. Hell, he'd already been struck. The venomous words spread through Zack's veins whether Brody knew it or not.

He should leave. Let Brody cool off. He was being an unreasonable jackass and only getting angrier. And his communication skills really sucked. Zack should go. Come back tomorrow when Brody wasn't looking to attack whoever came into sight.

Brody's gaze jerked back up to Zack's. "What?" he snapped. "What do you want? I have work to do."

In the end, that was what finally made Zack snap back. He'd be damned if he was going to stand there and be dismissed so openly—again.

"No. You have a job to *lose* and relationship to sabotage, and you're doing a damn fine job of both."

"What?" Brody pushed himself out of the chair to stand again.

"You think I don't know destructive behavior when I see it? You think you can stand there and say whatever you want just because I'm a nice guy? Grow the fuck up, Brody. You see what you want to see and believe what you want to, not the truth. The truth is I care about you, and you can't deal with it because you can't accept that a *man* cares about you. Not a mother, not a wife. *Me.* But all you see is interference when really, it's me giving a shit about you. What if they suspend you for messing in the case again? You said it could happen. Maybe you have good reason to risk it, but I wouldn't know, because you won't tell me. You're deliberately being a jackass to run me off because life just got real. I've had it done to me before, so I know how it feels. Got the therapy bills to prove it too."

Brody bowed up, the same body language Zack hadn't seen since they were first in PT. Brody had a way about him that surely intimidated a lot of people, but Zack knew it for what it was. A defense mechanism. Brody didn't scare him.

"Excuse me?"

"Quit acting like you can't hear me when I'm standing right here speaking English."

Brody stiffened further, like he was ready for a back-alley brawl. Last time Zack was here, he'd gotten that very same treatment. Right before Brody kissed him and then made him come.

Zack knew tonight that wasn't happening. "You don't want to talk about your feelings?" he asked. "Fine. Be a walled-up asshole. You were that way when I met you. You don't want me asking questions and caring? Don't want to talk about your job or any real-life issues that matter? Too bad. I can't just pretend like we're fuck buddies and tell myself every day that my concern and valid opinions don't mean shit to you. You are not going to talk down to me or screw your career and possibly life and expect me not to say anything or have any opinion at all because I'm your gay lover. *Fuck. That.*"

Brody's eyes widened slightly before going right back into target mode. It was meant as a warning, but Zack was already on a roll with no stop in sight.

"You've already been demoted, and now you're talking suspension? Getting fired? And I'm supposed to stand here and not care because I'm what? Just the flavor of the month? Maybe everyone else cowers to all this fury you dish out. Maybe they won't say shit to you, but I'm not everyone else, and you know it. You say that kind of crap to me because you think you can. Try to run me off like I don't matter. Well, fuck you. *I matter.*"

"You should." Brody's eyes narrowed, the gray almost as dark as charcoal. Unforgiving. "But I didn't ask you here, Zack. I didn't want you inserted in the middle of this part of my life, and I didn't ask you to fix my problems."

"Yeah, I got that message loud and clear." He was being dismissed. Brody didn't want a boyfriend. A partner. He wanted a boy toy to play with, then put back in the closet so he wouldn't have to mix real life with a relationship and all the complicated details that went along with both. Zack knew this going in too. He knew this would blow up on him, and he'd gone and fell for Brody anyway.

But he was not going to be Brody's convenient secret. All good for the sex and good times but hidden away during real life or really bad times, missing for stuff that mattered. He'd been there and sworn he wouldn't do that to himself again. He already hated himself for getting involved with Brody when he knew he wasn't out. Now he hated himself for loving the idiot.

"You know what, Brody? You can stay in here in the dark with your whiskey and slept-in hair, and you can beat and fuck up your life all by yourself. You're so stuck in the habit of denying the truth and hating yourself for it, you miss what's right in front of you anyway, so why should I bother? You obviously don't need someone who cares about you, because they'd only cramp your self-destructive bullshit. So you know what? Keep the phone off, because I sure as hell will."

Brody's eyes had lost some of their fury, but he hadn't softened and he wasn't backing down. Zack had to get away. His chest constricted with the dismissal, and his heart was pounding with the reminder of exactly how easy he was to throw away.

It was too late to get out of this with his heart intact, but it was time to back up. He refused to be a shameful secret or a burden for caring. He sure as hell wasn't going to be the toss-away fling, not when he already filled the role of toss-away son.

The walls started to close in as he turned for the door. He couldn't feel his feet move as he reached it, jerked it open. All he felt was the deafening pain that Brody didn't get it. He felt himself breaking inside, because, despite everything, Zack really, really *did*.

No amount of running would relieve the ripping pain that was tearing him apart inside as he somehow made it down the stairs. But he would. He'd go home, tie on his running shoes, and run until he couldn't breathe. Then he'd truly fall apart.

CHAPTER SEVENTEEN

Brody blinked against the hard, dry pillow, rolling his face into it for comfort. It wasn't a pillow at all.

"Shit." Brody pushed himself to sit up straight at his kitchen table, plucking a sticky note off his cheek. He'd finally managed to doze off after the night from hell. Too bad he hadn't managed to make it to his bed. He unfolded himself to stand; every bone seemed to crack as he stretched. He shook out his knee, still conscious of working out the pins and needles before putting weight on it. But damn, it was in good shape, considering. Good shape because of...

He grumbled, shuffling to the shower. He was not going to think about Zack or last night or what he'd said or what Zack had said or any of it.

"Fuck it," he said to his haggard reflection. It was never going to go anywhere anyway. Not with someone like him. Truth was, Zack deserved better, and they both knew it. It would've gone this way eventually. He'd only saved them both further pain and time.

Right now he had to focus on this case. This case that would always be his, no matter what the captain said or who Griggs had to blow to steal it from under him. This killer was Brody's to catch.

He turned his face into the hot spray, cringing at the pain but needing it to wake up. He had work to do. Ten-minute shower and two cups of coffee later, he was back at his table, files out before him.

The answer was here. But he had to see it. He hadn't yet, so maybe it was time to look at it differently.

He picked up the faces of the five girls and placed them out in front of him. Next with the crime-scene locations. All girls aged twenty to twenty-three, all killed on campus, sometime between two and four in the morning. All had a relatively low blood-alcohol level, all strangled with leather like any common belt and lots of power behind it, little to no defensive wounds. Made sense with a big, male attacker that they all knew. Yet there were no common friends, family, or coworkers who fit that profile.

He closed his eyes and pinched his nose, taking slow, deep breaths as he resisted the urge to throw something. He'd been staring at those bright faces for his entire career. And he had nothing to say to them. Nothing to reassure them of justice or peace. Nothing. The murderer breezed in, took their lives, and then breezed out.

A jolt of pain sprang from his shoulder and up to his neck. He groaned as he reached back and started rubbing at it. He lacked finesse. Zack laughed at him when he'd offered a massage, said that he tried to growl the pain away. Zack always had strong, sure hands that took the ache away as easily as he smiled.

Zack.

"Hell." Brody let his hand drop to the table with a thump. Of course Zack was absolutely right. Brody *was* a walled-up asshole whose confinement was his own creation. He couldn't see what was there because it didn't fit into his preconceived notions of how he should be. But he'd never denied that. They'd both known that going into...what they went into. A...relationship.

He'd never denied being scared of the truth about himself, so he did everything he could not to see it.

"You only see what you want to see instead of the truth," Zack had told him.

Brody shoved his chair back. He was not about to sit there and fixate on what Zack had said. When he moved to push himself up, he also pushed a third of the files onto the floor.

"Dammit."

Papers fluttered down, some sweeping wide and escaping into the den, the majority landing under the table.

"You're so stuck in the habit of denying the truth and hating

yourself for it, you miss what's right in front of you anyway."

Brody stared at the fallen files, cussing them once more before moving toward the kitchen. His foot crunched on something, and he winced. He might be a mess, but he really was a perfectionist when it came to his paperwork.

What if Zack was right? In more than just his personal life, Brody tended toward tunnel vision when shit got real. He could at least admit that much now.

So what was he not seeing? In all of his controlled environment, all the rules and regs, what had he missed? What was the one thing he'd assumed as truth from the start of this case? That it was a big guy the victim knew but not the boyfriend. What if it was a guy she didn't know?

But then why wouldn't she fight? It didn't make sense, because any woman would defend herself to whatever level she could. She wasn't knocked out. No concussions. Some big-ass, strange man approached one of the vics at night, she's a woman alone, she'd go on guard automatically. It's nighttime, maybe she's a little drunk, if a guy gets too close or she felt cornered, she'd move toward light and people.

These killings weren't far from the heart of the campus, which was right downtown. He had the brass ones to leave the body at the actual crime scene too. The guy was either stupid or very confident.

Wait...

The guy.

What if it wasn't a guy? The victims might not think to be on the defensive. Let their guard down.

What if it was another girl? Even if it didn't work with forensics. These women were jacked up as they were choked. No big struggle, a definite advantage in size and strength. But still...what if?

He entertained the notion further, let the scenario roll out in his mind like his father used to.

"Play it out in your head, son. You've got to think like a predator to catch one."

A female. She approaches the victims and they feel safe.

What's to fear if she's just like you?

Except she's a killer.

That didn't explain the power. She'd have to be a big fucking woman to get the angle and force to kill these girls quickly. It didn't make physical sense or even seem possible.

"Shit." Brody pinched the bridge of his nose, trying to get his worn eyes to focus.

A scribble in the corner of a page caught Brody's eye because it was his writing from ages ago, because his writing had only looked that good when he'd started the job. It had gotten progressively *interesting* over the last few years.

His note was a comment on whether the girls had any of the same classes. They had a few in common, during different semesters, but nothing had panned out from that line of questioning. Plus this last victim, she went to a completely different college.

Brody remembered looking at the teachers and TAs for the classes they had in common, but they'd both been women, so that line of thinking had been dropped. Something tripped in his mind, and he reached for the info on the most recent girls. Classes, dorms, majors.

It was a liberal arts school, so they all took the basics of the college. English, History, Art, Sociology. That was no help. The one that stood out was Philosophy. Damn. It'd kill him slowly to sit through Philosophy.

He flipped through the pages. Same professor for the second and third victim, not the first and obviously not the latest. Still, maybe there was a TA Brody hadn't looked at yet, a janitor, somebody from the building they all frequented. If the latest victim frequented the campus, it was worth a shot. What the hell else did he have to go on?

"Fuck it." He stacked up the papers and slid them in the file.

Paper only told you so much. Now that he was open to the seemingly improbable equal-opportunity killer, he needed to get eyes on where the crimes had happened. If it was a woman, she couldn't have just strolled up behind them. He needed to see in order to figure it out. He trusted his instincts. That was, he trusted them when they weren't clouded by his blind stubbornness.

He changed into some slacks, a button-down, and grabbed his jacket, mind and body humming with an inner truth. There was something here. Something he had to see and hear and touch before he could grab the full picture.

He drove around most of the day. He went by every crime scene, taking mental images along with the pictures in the files. He made a stop at the university offices, spoke with administration, asked for information regarding the classes and who had been running them. The class had been run by two professors during the time frame; the first was seventy-five when she retired, and the second, Ms. Bathory, who had taken over after the first death.

Nothing solid, but it was a start.

Brody clutched at the information, squinting at the address as he climbed into his car. It wasn't far, just a few blocks from the main campus. Definitely within striking distance.

He pulled up outside the well-maintained but old row house. Common sense nagged at the back of his conscience. He should call up Lamont, get him out here. He wasn't supposed to be on this case, and Zack was absolutely right about the possibility of this all exploding in his face. He should've said as much last night instead of acting like a tyrant.

Brody tapped the steering wheel and reached over for his badge in the glove box, his gun digging into his side as he pulled back. He couldn't turn back time, and right now he had to focus.

There was no harm in just asking a few questions. Brody just wanted to talk to her, get his sensors out about the type of person she was. Then he could give a new, viable direction to Lamont and feel he wasn't letting them down. Letting the girls down.

He sat, fully aware he was hesitating. The cool weight of his badge pressed into his palm, thumbs running over the letters.

He rubbed at his knee, feeling the groove of his scar beneath the dress pants. Regardless of what he tried to convince himself of with, new leads, devotion, whatever...this was stupid. Zack's worried face filled his mind, and he huffed out a sigh. Torn between his drive to see this through and what he felt for Zack and knew to be the truth, he reached for his phone.

He sent a quick message to Lamont.

Following up potential lead at 333 Wentworth. Professor from victims' classes. Meet me. I'll give you my notes.

Brody's thumb hovered over Send. Damn. Lamont would give him so much shit over this. He preemptively added, *Don't bitch. Just drive.*

He hit Send and jumped out of the car, fumbling for his notepad and pen. His dad had always said that the notepad was as important to a cop as a gun. Talking to people, seeing where they trip up, and where their stories changed. That was a cop's bread and butter.

"Learn everything they don't want you to know by watching them react," his dad used to say. It was comforting to hear his voice as he walked up the front path.

Brody tapped politely on the door. Deep breath, relax the shoulders, disarming face. No need to put her on edge at the start. *"Make them nervous only when you need it. Until then, put them at ease."*

The door opened to reveal a woman, late thirties, tall, eyeing him skeptically as she straightened her vest. "May I help you?"

"Ms. Bathory?"

"Yes."

Brody pulled out his badge, holding it open. "I'm Detective Douglas Brody from Charleston Police Department. I was hoping I could ask you a few questions."

Ms. Bathory kept her hand on the door. "What is this about, Detective?"

She wasn't hostile, but she certainly wasn't warm and welcoming. Either she had something against cops or just a chip on her shoulder in general. Perfect.

"I'm investigating the murders of the young women at the university. I believe you work there?"

Brody watched for the fine nuances of her expression, blips in the calm facade. Nothing. She barely blinked. "I've heard.

Horrible news. A few of them were in my class."

Not just a few. Try all but one. Brody's stomach turned; something was off, and she hadn't even invited him in yet. Time to gain some trust.

"Yes. We're looking within the student body, and I was wondering if I may ask you a few questions, maybe gain some information or insight we may have missed?"

Ms. Bathory frowned, giving Brody's non-police-issue car a quick glance. "Detectives don't work with partners anymore?"

"Usually. But I'm off duty." *And basically freelancing and walking a fine line that could get my ass reprimanded.* "Thought I'd drop by on my way home."

She smiled, nodded, and pulled open the door. "How very devoted of you. Of course. Please come in. Excuse the mess; it's finals for the summer sessions."

Mess my ass, Brody thought as he followed the professor into the living room. Everything was clean lines and bare walls. Out on the dining table lay neat piles of papers in a perfect row, almost like it had been measured with a ruler. Yeah sure, that wasn't creepy.

Ms. Bathory indicated the couch, sitting carefully on the opposite side. "What would you like to know?"

Brody handed the professor the smiling head shots of each of the girls before taking out his note pad. "The victims all took Philosophy 101. Around the death of the first girl, the class was initially run by your predecessor and then you accepted the job two years later."

"This is correct. I was assisting Mrs. Carson while working on my doctorate, accepted the position after her retirement." The professor shifted through them before laying the photos in her lap. "I recognize some of these girls."

"Did you notice anyone they hung out with? Any common classmates or friends? Any senior students providing tutoring within the class?"

Ms. Bathory shook her head slowly. "Not that I was aware of. Teachers' aides and professors rarely gain insight into the intimate relationships of their students." She chuckled. "Though maybe the relationship to their concept of study."

Brody huffed a laugh. "True." He tapped his pen against his pad. "What about your teacher's aides? Any interaction between the girls and any TAs you've had working for you? Maybe someone who's been involved in the classes? Had potential contact with the four victims?"

Ms. Bathory sighed and shook her head again. "No. I'm sorry. I've had a few TAs who have come and gone. Philosophy isn't exactly a subject people are drawn toward." She handed back the photos. "I wish I could be more helpful."

There had to be something he'd missed. The commonality was the campus, downtown, and this class was all that stood out. His gut told him there was something here, and, while guilty of sometimes missing the big picture, he trusted his gut. Lamont would chide him and tell him that his gut was *not* evidence, but it was.

The perfect and detached facade the professor exuded put Brody's teeth on edge. She didn't have a connection to all four girls, but there was shit-all else evidence wise. He'd just have to probe further. Keep looking. Keep asking. Forget that he shouldn't be doing either.

"What about yourself? You say that you recognized some of the girls. Is there anything you can tell me about *your* relationship with them?"

Ms. Bathory pressed her lips together. "I teach a lot of students, Detective. I can place a few faces, but that's all. I rarely have any interaction with them outside lectures and assisting the few who are genuinely interested in the course work. I can't say I remember talking to any of the girls in the photos."

Brody instantly felt the change in the air. The hostility she tried to hide under a veneer of calm was bleeding through. His instincts, honed from his experience on the street, blared red with warning. It was something that no cop academy could teach you but was something that all cops innately learned. A sixth sense sounded like bullshit, but there was no other analogy that fit. And currently his sixth sense was kicking him in the ass.

He breathed into his muscles and relaxed. He had to keep the pressure on but appear relaxed. Sound innocent but dog her with questions.

"All the girls shared one common class, except the first victim. There must be *something* you remember. Someone suspicious?"

The professor tapped her hands once against the arms of the chair. Finality. "I'm sorry, Detective Brody, but I can't think of anything else of relevance." She stood up. "I'm sorry to have to end this, but I have a lot of reading and papers to grade before tomorrow."

Brody nodded and stood up too, tucking away his notebook. Not much to go on, certainly nothing to warrant a search, but maybe a new lead for Lamont. He could give his old partner his notes, get him to maybe look into the TAs. He could always requestion, catch her in a lie.

"Oh," he piped up. "One more thing before I go. If it's not too much trouble, could I have the contact details for your prior and current TAs?"

The professor stopped, her gaze meeting his in a stare-off. "Why would you require that? I'd assumed you ruled them out as suspects."

Again, aggression but beneath a calm exterior. Brody kept his tone casual, like this was all an afterthought. "Yeah, we have, but it never hurts to see if they have any ideas. You know, something you may have missed."

She cleared her throat. There was a beat of silence and then a forced, polite smile. "Of course, I have their numbers in my office. One moment." She left the room and headed down the hallway.

His phone buzzed in his pocket. Lamont.

Don't you dare. Don't Bitch me! Dammit, Brody.

The second text vibrated through.

Hill will mount your head on his wall. On my way now. Have your ass ready when I get there.

Brody smirked, hearing every word in an annoyed but familiar baritone. He texted back. *Hurry up, old man.*

It felt good. Finally a new stretch of possibilities on a case that'd plagued him almost as long as his career. He slid his phone back into his pocket and tapped his fingers against his thigh.

Damn, how long did it take? It'd felt like a damn while.

He waited another moment, not wanting to come across as the impatient asshole he could be. A few more minutes went by and nothing.

He took a few steps forward, leaning to let his voice carry down the hallway. "Ms. Bathory?"

No response. He called again, feeling his voice echo in the suddenly silent house.

Something dark slid into his stomach, setting his nerves alight. The low-running tension he'd been feeling since he'd arrived cranked into fifth gear. His mind raced, flicking through his options as his hand came to his gun.

He slowed his breathing and tried to think rationally. Logically.

He couldn't just go after her, gun drawn. He shouldn't even be here. She'd disappeared into the house and wasn't responding, but it could be innocent.

One of three things was true. One, she was the Strangler. Two, the Strangler had gotten into the house and taken her out because she was involved. Three, the poor woman was just busy in another room of the house, looking for some phone numbers.

Talk about different ends of a spectrum.

Yet all the officer safety classes warned of being prepared and not letting yourself be backed into a corner. Cautious in unfamiliar surroundings. Have backup. Be safe. He reached for his phone, keeping his eye on the hallway and lowering his voice.

"Lamont," he said as soon as his buddy answered. "I'm going to need you to speed up that ETA, you copy?"

Lamont's tone was direct, concerned. Because he understood. "You all right? We need backup?"

"No. Might be nothing." And he was going to get in so much shit if they went blasting in and the poor woman was faultless. "But something tells me otherwise. Pull up out front. Come in quiet."

"I'll be two minutes."

Brody hung up and reached for his gun. Clicking off the safety and holding it steady, he waited. Time stretched out like a highway, making each moment tick by, heavy and suffocating. The images flashing through Brody's mind made waiting hurt like a bitch.

There was a muffled grunt and a *thud*.

Brody raised his gun in the direction of the noise.

"Ms. Bathory!" he yelled again.

Silence. What if she had hurt herself or was being attacked? Concern for a citizen was cause enough. Brody shifted to where he could see down the shadowed hallway and pursued.

He heard the faint noise of tires crunching as a car pulled to a stop. The vise on his chest lessened with the knowledge Lamont was here. He flicked his eyes back to see Lamont's tall frame silently climbing the front stairs. He put his finger to his mouth in silent warning. If this was something bad, he didn't want her to think he had backup. Put her on the back foot.

Lamont sidled up beside him, gun also drawn. The surge of familiarity and trust bolstered Brody in ways no one besides another cop could ever understand.

"I was questioning her about the girls," he whispered. "Asked for the TAs' contacts, and she went into the other room to retrieve them. Been over ten minutes and no response."

"That way?" Lamont nodded toward the hallway.

"Yeah." Brody steadied his grip on his GLOCK. "I'll go, you cover."

His heart thumped as he moved down the hallway, Lamont in step behind. They methodically and quietly searched the rooms, his clearance tactics running commentary in his mind. Minimize time in the doorway, slice the pie. The house remained quiet, Brody's ears straining for any movement.

They reached the end room, searched and cleared. Where the fuck was she?

Lamont turned to him from the cupboard with a similar look on his face. "Back door?" he whispered.

There was another *thump* and a grunt, from right above them. Brody moved to the hallway and looked up to see a pull-down access to the attic. He slowly pulled the door down; the ladder was flimsily attached like it was makeshift. It was a steep climb and no light switch, only the flicking of light from the roof exhaust fans.

Fuck it. He was going to have to go up there. He lowered the ladder and cast a look back at Lamont, who only nodded at him, steadying his gun.

He'd barely popped his shoulders through the gap when he felt something slip over his neck and his airway clamped down, literally stealing his breath. He lashed out, hands grabbing the ladder to fight against it, but all it did was tighten the noose. The rope pulled up, tugging him farther into the hole, before his survival instincts gave in and he went with it. The need for air was too great.

His head reeled as the skin at his neck burned. The rope cut into his skin as he was pulled completely into the attic, and he kept thinking, *How?*

His calf scraped along a corner as his feet were dragged in. He tried to flip up. The sound of the rope brushing against the wooden eave groaned as the noose grabbed tighter.

She had him leveraged up over...something. He was being choked *up*, and he fought at the rope, trying to loosen it. He managed to roll his body, kicking out with the tip of his foot, but he only rattled the ladder against its perch.

"Brody!"

Brody's vision rolled as he heard a "Shit!" behind him. His vision dimmed in and out, adrenaline coursing through his veins as he tried to get his fingers underneath the rope.

But his vision wasn't dim enough to blank out the flash of steel.

He lurched back in time to miss the daggerlike scissors aimed at his chest but not enough to miss the slice of fire through his biceps. She was panicking now; she hadn't expected Lamont.

To buy Lamont time to get to him, Brody grabbed tighter at the rope around his neck. He took a deep breath, pulled up with his hands, and swung himself back to try to put her off-balance. There was a cry of pain and the rope slackened, just enough for a gasping breath.

Lamont stood over them, voice deep and terrifying. "Drop them! Off the rope! Get on the floor. Now!"

Brody only heard muffled words exchanged as the rope went slack and he fell completely to the ground. He drew in gasping breaths and blinked his eyes to focus, blood rushing to his head as his ears turned back on.

There was moving around, his vision sparkling with the return of air.

"You all right?" Lamont kept his gun on the professor.

Brody blinked, his vision clearing, his neck and chest burning like a motherfucker.

"I'm..." He coughed, his voice sounding awful. "I'm all right."

"Good." Lamont quickly tossed Brody his cuffs. "Because there's no way I'm not letting you have the honors."

Brody nodded, blinking again as he pushed away the leather rope. He crawled over to the left side of the attic opening, where the professor lay prone. Placing a knee on her back, he snapped the cuffs into place. He felt his strength waning, so he sat, leaning his weight on her. He felt like the noose was still squeezing, so there was no way in hell he was giving her a chance to move. He could hear Lamont's voice over the radio asking for a unit. Brody looked up as he felt Lamont touch his sliced arm. He couldn't stop the grimace. She'd gotten him good.

Lamont grabbed at his other hand and pushed it against the wound. "Keep some pressure on it." He stood back up, requesting an RA, but when he snapped his radio back into place, his eyes widened. "Brody."

Brody followed his gaze to the back wall of the attic. A map. Pictures, newspaper clippings. A long row of leather ropes, belts, and the most recent girl's photos from the *Post* and *Courier*.

With the sirens starting to wail in the distance, Brody could only croak out, "Well, fuck me."

———※———

Brody swore, gripping the bumper of the ambulance, ready to rip it off with his good arm as the RA officer rinsed the knife wound in his other arm with something that burned like fire.

"Yeah, this'll need stitches." She pressed a pad over it and started wrapping. "Do you need a ride?"

Brody shook his head. "I don't have time. Can't you just stitch it here?"

The officer looked amused. "Does this look like a hospital to you?" She tightened the bandage. "That arm needs stitching, so either you come with us or get one of your colleagues to drive you."

"I'll take him." Lamont walked up, tilting Brody's face to look at his neck. "And don't think about arguing with me."

"Wouldn't dream of it." He batted Lamont's hand away.

The RA officer tidied up and left them to it. Lamont watched her go before he sat down. He folded his arms and leaned against the side of the door.

"Damn. I've never been gladder in my life to be swept up in one of your shit storms." There was a long moment of silence; Brody looked up to see the fear in Lamont's eyes. "You would be dead if you hadn't called me."

Brody gingerly touched the burn around his neck. "Yeah. I know." He would have been. He'd be dead along with every one of those girls.

"Found the latest vic's info in Bathory's attic too. She was a friend of her TA's. I think when you got nosy on the TA lead, that's when she freaked. Scare a rabid animal into a corner and—"

"They'll bite."

"Yep."

Bite and kill. Dead if he hadn't heeded the concern of someone who cared. Dead, and who would he have left behind?

Zack.

The emotion that built behind Brody's eyes sparked hot and painful. He'd have gone out, swept up in a case that had been plaguing him his entire career, and been a dumb-ass. Gone after her alone because he couldn't let it go. Because he never allowed himself to let it go.

And Zack would have spent the rest of his life not knowing how much he meant, because Brody couldn't let go of the bullshit jail he'd put himself inside.

His heart pounded with the urgency to find Zack. To wrap his arms around him, hold his tall-ass moose frame, fingers digging into that soft, long hair that almost swept his stupid broad shoulders and feeling warm, sure hands hug him right back.

But he'd been such an asshole. He'd pushed the only good thing in his life right out the door. Because he was scared. Because he couldn't allow himself something real.

What if he'd lost Zack for good?

The heat burned harder than the wound around his neck. Brody slammed his hand down against the bumper. "*Fuck!*"

He closed his eyes and prayed to every fucking thing out there that he could get Zack back. Somewhere out there, the scales had to be balanced. Surely something deemed him worthy. His mind swirled, pain and loss building a lump in his throat. But a warm, comforting hand landed on his shoulder, brought him back to reality.

"Brody." Lamont squeezed. "It's okay. You caught her. You did it. She'd be still out there, plotting her next life to take, and now she won't. It's over."

It grounded him. Only just. "But I fucked up. I should have listened." His voice was gravelly, the emotion causing his already swollen vocal cords to grate.

There was a fond, good-natured chuckle. "Yeah, well. I can't say that the captain won't be pissed, but it's a good outcome. I don't think you'll be in too much shit." Lamont gave him a little shake, then let go. "At most you'll get a paid holiday. And man, you *need* it. You look like hell."

Brody laughed. Forced, but it relieved some of the tension.

"*And* you need to stop getting injured on the job. People will start to think I don't do anything."

Brody looked up and caught the glint in Lamont's eyes as he huffed out another laugh.

"You've finally caught the sonuvabitch that's been plaguing you since you were a fresh-faced probie." Lamont gestured to Brody's half-broken body. "So why do you look like you ran over someone's puppy?"

Startlingly true. Except he'd run over his own puppy.

"Because I fucked up. I mean, I *really* fucked up."

"Yeah, so you mentioned. And I *told* you, Hill won't—"

"Not the captain," he interrupted. How could he explain? "Someone... It's someone else."

A dark eyebrow rose. "Someone as in, *someone?* Someone important?"

Only everything that mattered. But he couldn't bring himself to say it. Not when it wasn't guaranteed that Zack would even be his someone back anymore. "Yeah."

Lamont moved to stand in front of Brody, arms crossed, eyes clearly in interrogation mode. "So who is—"

Brody stopped him with a hand. "I'll tell you. Take me to fix this shit up first." He shrugged his wrapped arm. "I have some stuff to sort out, but I *will* tell you. Deal?"

Lamont stared at him a beat longer before nodding and pulling out his keys. "Deal. But only because you're the walking wounded. Let's go."

CHAPTER EIGHTEEN

Zack tightened the knot on the cleat, pulling the boat in closer to the dock. Like it'd protect *Mary* from unexpectedly sinking in a freak act of nature.

She wouldn't sink, though. He was pretty sure. No, he was completely sure. He was just freaking out a bit.

Zack stood up straight and shook out his shoulders. He'd spent far too much time checking and rechecking *Mary*. He'd performed all the necessary tests, and she passed swimmingly. She was watertight and just needed him to man up and get in. And actually sail her.

That really vivid dream with him sailing and *Mary* bucking him out into churning seas with sharks had made him have a long conversation with her this morning about fair play. He'd be an awesome captain if she didn't try to drown him. It was a good deal.

Maybe he might check the sailing checklist again.

If he was honest with himself, he'd accept that he'd been ignoring the world and obsessing over pointless concerns like *Mary's* safety since his fight with Brody.

It'd been two days, and Zack prided himself on the fact he'd kept his cell off. Not checking it, not even looking at it. Instead he checked and double-checked his boat. Anything was better than reliving that moment. Picking it apart. Worrying over how much of it was Brody's part and what, if any, role he played in their demise.

For now, he was in Zack-avoidance happy land and fully

intended to stay there until the pain of missing Brody didn't feel like he was dying.

He suspected it'd only take a few hundred years.

He shook his head and refocused. No. It was his last day off, and there was no way in hell he was going to think about Brody. Or acknowledge the aching hole in his chest.

Nope.

He pulled his *My other car is a boat* sailing cap down on his head and checked *Mary* over one last time. Then there'd be nothing left but to untie her and push off into the deep blue yonder.

And then freak out his yonder.

The dock was relatively deserted for a late Friday afternoon that promised a beautiful sunset. A few older guys were setting up their fishing lines at the end of the dock, playing cat and mouse with the seagulls as they baited their hooks. One family ushered their laughing kids and an army of bags down the dock and onto one of the moored boats.

Zack started going through one of his bags, pulling things out, lining them up on the weathered wood, going through his mental checklist one last time. It was peaceful, relaxing. Getting his sail Zen on.

Which was exactly why he nearly dropped his roll of Kevlar tape into the water when two black-leather-shoe-clad feet came to a stop in front of him.

He knew only one person who wore shoes like that.

"Zack."

It was Brody.

Zack clutched at the bag, taking a deep breath before he looked up. He would be strong. He would not lose it. He would calmly tell Brody he was not interested in anything he had to say. That it was better this way, because neither of them could be the person the other needed.

He slowly raised his eyes, scanning over the well-filled-out pants, the slightly wrinkled undershirt, the recently shaved face, the horrid bruising and burn marks around his—

Zack leaped to his feet, all his resolve evaporated. "What

the hell happened to you?"

Brody put out his hands, attempting to placate him. "It's fine, Zack. I'm fine."

"Like hell it's fine!" Against his will, he was suddenly up in Brody's space, hands gentle on his face, making him tilt his chin up to get a better look. The red, raw mark went all the way around. Like someone had tried to strangle him. His left arm was also bandaged around the curve of his biceps. A hint of old blood seeped through the white.

"Wh-what happened?" he asked, even as his brain starting clicking the answer into its proper slot.

"It's not important, it's—" Brody stopped. Cut himself off firmly, like he'd caught himself. "No. No, you *should* know. I want you to." He took a deep breath and met Zack's gaze. "I caught the killer, the Strangler, the one I've been chasing."

"Who was it?"

"A professor at the university. A fucking philosophy professor of all things, and I may not have put two and two together if not for thinking about what you'd said when...when we argued. But you were right, sometimes I don't see the obvious. I finally made a connection, though, and I went after her. I went off on my own and would have gotten myself killed, except again, I remembered what you'd said. That I was being an idiot." Brody rubbed at his bandage. "I called my partner last minute, and he saved me." Brody moved his hands to Zack's upper arms and squeezed gently. "Your concern saved me."

Zack blinked at him. "She...she tried to kill you?"

"Yeah, but she didn't." Brody said it like it wasn't unusual for someone to try to kill him. And in his profession, it probably wasn't. "She didn't succeed because you made me think, and sitting there, watching that murderer get hauled away, you'd think..." Brody blinked too. He swallowed, his Adam's apple bobbing with thinly held emotion. "I was relieved. For those girls, for those I may have saved. But then I felt...empty. Blank. I finally caught her, and I felt *nothing*. Because all I could think about was what if I'd died and you never knew."

Zack's heart was beating too hard at just the thought. It made his hands tingle. "I...I would've seen it. On the news."

Brody shook his head like he was holding back a smile. What the hell was there to smile about?

"No. Not about that. You never would've known how I really felt. About you."

His gaze caught on Brody's neck, on the angry red mark encircling it. Everything he was saying, both of them standing there, it all began to feel surreal.

Brody had almost died. He was talking about feelings...about how he felt *about Zack...*

Zack reminded himself to breathe. He didn't know what to say, and his mouth was too dry to form words. He'd figured if Brody ever did turn up, it would be to maybe say *thanks for the fun*, but definitely *fuck the hell off*.

This? He hadn't expected.

Brody moved closer, cautiously. "I've been a complete ass, and you were right. You called me on my bullshit, and you had every reason. I was a scared, stupid little shit and—" He tightened his hold on Zack's arms. "I was wrong to push you away. My job, what I do, it isn't easy, and it won't be easy to be with you, but you're too damn important to give up. I know that, hell, I knew that, but...I...I've lived my life by this fucked-up set of rules for so long—rules I made for myself because of who I thought I had to be in order to make it. I couldn't just stop living that way. I didn't know how. It took nearly getting strangled to realize they're *my* rules now. It should be what *I* want. Not what someone else thinks I should be." There was a huff of a laugh, but Zack could see it was hollow. Brody was trying to keep it together. "I always knew I was a cop, but I've also always known I was gay. I just... I didn't want to be, because I knew it'd crush my father, and that had to make me wrong somehow. Maybe undeserving of the badge but definitely undeserving of love. Then...you came along. You proved me wrong. I know you loved me, and I'm sorry I fucked that up."

Zack looked into those sincere gray eyes, and everything he had told himself, everything he'd decided, fell away. His fear for Brody and what he'd been through, what he went through every day in his job, was very real. But if Brody was brave enough to face his fears, then Zack would be damned if he'd be any less.

He couldn't stop himself as he launched forward and swept Brody into his arms. He pressed their bodies tight together, reminding himself that Brody was safe and real in his arms. He cupped Brody's head as he turned his face into the familiar smell of his neck. And Brody clutched him right back. No flinch at the very public arena, just a warm hand resting on his back, pulling Zack irrevocably closer into his arms.

"I want this, Brody." Zack spoke against Brody's ear. "Call me a stupid moose—"

"You are a stupid moose." The voice was equally gravelly with emotion.

Zack laughed, warmth rising up his chest with the feeling

"But you're my stupid moose. And that's why I love you."

Zack pulled back to look Brody in the face. He took a step back while he still had the power to manage it. "I... God, Brody, you know I love you too, and that's why I...I can't go back to the way it was. I want to do this, but if we do this, I want the whole deal. I can't be casual. Not with you. I want the good things *and* this scary shit. When the crap of life hits the fan, I want to be there for you. I'm not going to be your dirty secret, and I'm not going back in the closet. I've been there, done that, and no way in hell am I going to do that again. So if you can't—"

"Hey." Brody cut him off, one of those small, rare smiles brightening his face. "I wouldn't have come after you if I didn't intend to go forward. I mean...I'm not going to be jumping on the nearest pride float anytime soon. I'm not going to hide from this anymore either."

Zack wanted to believe that. He wanted to forget all the hurts of the past and believe that Brody would love him the way they both deserved.

Brody lifted a hand to brush at Zack's hair, leaving it to cup his jaw. "So...how about this for starters?"

And on the dock, in the early evening with the sun dipping low, seagulls screeching and water splashing against the pier, people bustling, about to begin their weekend, Brody kissed Zack. He clutched at Zack's back and leaned in, pressing their mouths together, regardless of who might care to see.

It was soft and sweet, with a hint of more to come. It took a few beats before Zack could even respond. Because Brody was kissing him. In the open, with the sun warm on their faces.

Zack couldn't help the laugh that exploded against Brody's mouth. He dragged Brody closer, feeling his solid body, and thoroughly took his mouth. He kissed Brody with every inch of emotion he felt for his iron-willed cop. He cupped that gorgeous angular jaw and sipped at Brody's mouth like it was the beginning and ending of the universe.

Because screw everything, it totally was.

Zack broke the kiss and pulled back. He had to stop at some point or end up shoving Brody aboard and christening his boat in an entirely different way.

Matter of fact...it might be exactly what they needed.

Brody grinned. His face flushed like he knew what Zack was thinking, eyes shining in a way that Zack had only seen glimpses of once. Happiness.

"Well then, Captain." Brody licked at his lips and attempted to straighten his shirt...and his pants. "Aren't you going to show me how awesome a job I did?" He pointed to the painted hull.

"*You* did?" Zack shoved at him but had to smile. "You painted for a few hours. *Once.* I've worked my ass off to finish *Mary.*"

Brody angled his body to look behind Zack. "Doesn't look like it. Ass is still there." He climbed aboard, ignoring Zack's glare. "Come on. It'll be dark in a few hours, and then you'll really get anxious. Let's go."

Zack untied the rope and pushed off the dock. "You're pretty bossy considering you're not the captain. Don't make me keelhaul you."

Brody cracked up as he struggled into a life jacket. They continued to struggle, laugh, and swear their way through *Mary's* first sail.

They eventually got into a decent rhythm, *Mary* evening out as they hit smoother water, the wind warm with the last hour of the day's sun. Zach smiled at Brody from across the boat, mostly because he had the man he loved here with him and in his life, but also because he'd managed to tug a ridiculous cap onto Brody's head in the name of "protecting against skin cancer." It was too much fun seeing a man like Brody with a hat that read *Killing at sea is definitely going overboard.* Too much fun and inexplicably too sexy.

"We're going to need to anchor in that cove," Zack blurted.

"What?" Brody sat up straighter. "Why? Something up with *Mary*?"

He didn't bother stifling the laugh. "Something is about to be up all right, but *Mary* is fine."

Brody gave him a half-withering, half-hungry look. "You're impossible."

"And you love it."

They anchored in a small bay and lowered the sails. Zack's heart swelled with what they had, the fragility of life, and all the possibilities for the future. He reached for Brody, but Brody beat him to it, kissing him softly at first, with so much emotion Zack almost melted into the sea; then it grew heated and heavy, desperate from their near miss.

Zack urged him to sit back, clueless as to how they'd maneuver carnal activities on a sloop but knowing they'd figure out a way.

"Sailing is awesome," he said, panting against Brody's lips. Zack had one hand already under Brody's shirt, while the other jerked at the zipper of his pants.

Brody rumbled with a laugh. "Amazing what sex can do for your anxiety."

"Mmm. Shut up and let's get naked, or we'll be stuck out here in the dark."

"I can shine the flashlight while you steer us back." Brody grinned. "Whatever. I'll keep you safe."

And Zack knew he would. He was completely head over heels for this man, and for once in his life, he knew someone felt the same about him, no special conditions, catch, or sub-clause. It was simply the two of them, and it was exactly what he'd always wanted.

EPILOGUE

One month later...

B rody flipped his phone over and over in his hand, waiting on his lunch date.

Lunch. Date.

It sounded very relationship-esque, which still sent a spark of nerves and anxiety through him, but it was just Zack. They'd had plenty of meals together before now, but this was the first one they'd called a lunch "date." Both of them were breaking from work, taking a moment from the rush of their usual days to spend time with each other before going back, back to the other part of their lives, taking a small bit of the person they loved with them.

In Brody's book, it was a big fucking deal.

"Hey." Zack took the steps two at a time to the small porch of the restaurant. He wrapped his arms around Brody, squeezing tightly, and gave him a quick kiss on the lips. It wasn't a casual slap-on-the-back hug, nor was it a passionate embrace. It fell somewhere in between and was something they'd silently agreed on for in public.

They both knew who they were as individuals and to each other. Dip-kissing in a restaurant was never going to be their thing.

"Man, I'm starving. This place better have good Italian." Zack took the seat right beside him and scooted his chair in, a slow smile spreading across his face as their knees bumped, and Zack made sure to rub once for good measure and leave his leg pressed there.

"You're always starving," Brody told him. "And it's *excellent* Italian. I wouldn't be a regular otherwise. Two chicken parm specials," he told the waitress once she approached.

Zack glanced over at him, the look in his brown eyes softening. "And a water to drink," he added. "Awww. You ordered for me. That's so sweet and old-fashioned," he teased.

"Fuck off." Brody took a sip of his iced tea.

"So today is your first official day back with Lamont, right? How's it going?"

"Same as always," he was happy to report.

"Good. I am surprised I didn't get thrown over in favor of lunch with your infamous partner in crime. Bah dum dum." Zack hit an air cymbal.

"You've been waiting all morning to say that, haven't you?"

"All damn morning." He grinned, his teeth shining from the deep tan on his face. Zack and Brody had taken to sailing. And anchoring in coves. A lot.

Brody shook his head but was smiling too. "He's meeting his wife for lunch today or I might've."

"I'm wounded." Zack tapped his straw against the table to push it through the paper. "Maybe I can meet him some other time, though." His expression was one of casual small talk, but Brody knew his reaction and response mattered.

"Yeah. I want you to." Brody nodded. "You'll like Lamont; he's cool. And he'll think you're a fucking trip."

"That's because I *am* a fucking trip." Zack thanked the waitress once his water arrived and drank half of it in a few sips.

Their side salads arrived, and Brody was handing over his peperoncini peppers when his phone vibrated on the table. "Hey. What's up?" he answered, seeing Lamont's name.

"My appetite. Felicia canceled on me. You eat yet?"

Brody glanced over at Zack, who wasn't waiting on Brody before digging into his salad. It was one of the many things he'd learned about Zack. His Zack. The man waited on no one to eat. He also followed a detailed, drawn-out, getting-ready-for-bed ritual, and he never got road rage. Like…ever. Even in rush hour.

"I was just getting ready to. Want to join me?"

"Yeah. Where are you?"

"We're at Marie's."

Zack's shot a look at him, a bit of Italian dressing on his lips.

"I'll put in an order for you. Lasagna?"

"You know it. You said 'we'?"

Zack's brown eyes got impossibly wider as he licked at his lips. His many expressions showed practically every emotion, and Brody loved that about him. He rarely had to guess what Zack was thinking because it'd be written all over his face.

"Yeah. Hurry up. There's someone here I want you to meet."

Zack slowed down his chewing.

"Oh yeah? The someone you've skated around telling me about?"

"It is."

"Well *damn*. I'm on my way, then."

Brody ended the call and set his phone down, noting that his hands didn't shake.

"Was that...? Is he...?" Zack's eyebrows crept up into his hair.

"You're going to meet Lamont."

"Shit. Is there lettuce in my teeth?" He swiped at his face with the napkin and grinned as big as humanly possible.

Brody laughed but checked for him. "No. You look great."

"I didn't know I'd meet him today."

"Neither did I, but...today's as good as any, I guess."

Zack reached over and felt his forehead.

"Would you stop?" Brody grabbed his hand and laughed. He didn't let go right away. Instead he held it, brushing his thumb back and forth over Zack's knuckles. "I just... I need to do this. I *want* to do this, and the longer I put it off—it's going to gnaw at me. Plus, I think maybe I need you here to do this. If that makes any sense."

Zack studied him for a second and then smiled. "It does.

Aren't you nervous? I'm nervous. Why am I nervous? Now I'm sweating."

"I am too, but it is eighty degrees out here. Stop fidgeting, you'll make it worse." He let go of Zack's hand and straightened his shirt.

Their chicken parmesan arrived. Then so did Lamont. He stopped at the top of the stairs and looked at Brody. He looked at Zack. Then he looked back and forth between the two of them. Brody could feel all his nerves, all his anxiety ball into a hard knot in the center of his stomach.

"Well. Hey," Lamont finally said, taking the seat on the other side of Brody.

"Hey." Brody lifted his chin, feeling a lot like he was about to testify in front of a jury. "Lamont, this is Zack. He was my physical therapist after the knee surgery. Zack, this is Lamont."

Lamont was the first to stick out his hand, and Zack shook it.

"Your PT, huh?" Lamont asked.

"Yeah."

His partner nodded, staring down at the table before taking a sip of the tea they'd ordered him.

Brody could tell by Lamont's expression that he didn't have to explain any further. He'd said enough after getting choked nearly to death to make it pretty clear. But he had to say it anyway, if for no one else but himself.

"Zack is my...boyfriend."

That earned a small smile fighting to break free from Zack. The man radiated his feelings like a broadcast. At the moment it was like the after blast of a glee bomb.

"I kind of figured that much out." Lamont nodded. "Well...damn."

Brody waited, realized he was holding his breath, and made himself breathe.

Lamont finally looked up, looked at Zack and back to Brody. "I can't believe Felicia was right." He shook his head. "Dammit. I will never hear the end of this."

"Wh-what?"

Lamont rubbed his bare head. "Felicia. She's been saying for years, 'Honey, I'm telling you, that boy is gay.' I told her she was crazy, but she's always right." He held his hand out wide. "I just... I can't believe I didn't know."

"What?" Brody felt a little like a parrot, but this was not at all how he'd seen this going down.

"I can't believe I never knew. Or that you never *told* me. I mean, we've known each other how long? Almost ten years now. Been partners for how many of those years? I know you better than I know myself. Or I thought I did. Damn." He shook his head and actually looked hurt by it.

Brody shook his head. This wasn't really about Lamont.

"I didn't tell you...because I wasn't ready. And this isn't something that I want being everyone's business. It not something you can just—"

"Stop." Lamont put one big elbow on the table, rattling the flatware. "I'm doing this all wrong. Handling it poor as hell, and if I screw up, she'll chew my ass out later along with singing she told me so. Just...just give me a second. Okay?"

Brody closed his mouth and looked to Zack. Zack gave him a quick, reassuring nod.

After a beat of silence, Brody finally confessed. "I was scared to ever say anything to you. I didn't know how you'd react. Hell, I couldn't even admit it to myself until last month. It's my...experience that we aren't in the most gay-friendly work environment."

Lamont huffed a laugh before taking a deep breath and letting it out. "I just... I'm guessing this isn't new news, right? Not really?"

Brody nodded.

"Then I wish you would've felt okay to talk to me. Years ago. That's all."

Brody felt the knot start to loosen just a tad.

"Man, you know I..." Lamont glanced over at Zack and to Brody, his eyes shining. "You're like fucking *family* to me, okay? You've saved my ass so many times, and I've done the same for you. I don't care about what you do in your personal life or who you're with. I mean, not that I don't care as in 'I don't give a shit about them,' but I don't *care* care. Ah, you know what I mean."

"Yeah," Brody managed.

"I didn't have a clue. Even when Felicia said, well, she always has been smarter than me. So there you go." Lamont laughed, and the knot loosened a little more. He rubbed his hands over his head again and took another drink. "I'm not saying this won't..." He motioned back and forth between Brody and Zack. "Won't take me some... I'll have to, like, wrap my head around this, but damn, man. You're a brother to me. Always will be. This won't change that. Matter of fact, I owe you lunches now, you sorry ass. For maxing out your qualifying tests, right?"

Brody nodded. "Yeah. Thanks mostly to Zack."

Lamont smiled. "Then this one's on me."

"As I remember it, there are quite a few lunches on you."

His partner laughed. "You got me, man. Lunch*es*. Plural. It's all good."

Brody looked at his oldest friend and partner, laughing his usual booming laugh. Zack smiled in his relaxed way that reassured Brody things would be just fine. The knot in his stomach unfurled as he realized the two most important people in his life, the two he really cared about, also cared for him. Regardless of flaws, his belligerent stubbornness, and often downright bad attitude; even if he was and would always be far from perfect, he was accepted. Accepted and loved for who he really was.

"Yeah." Brody nodded. "It's all good."

And for the first time in his life, he really believed it.

❧The End❧

SAM B. MORGAN

Sam B. Morgan writes hot, contemporary M/M romance with gritty, complicated men. With a love of travel, settings like Los Angeles and Boston, and coastal cities like Charleston, South Carolina and San Francisco, California serve not only as backdrops, but supporting characters in his books. Sam enjoys fast cars and slow Sunday mornings. He lives in west Texas, with his longtime partner and their two dogs.

Learn more about Sam at http://sambmorgan.com/.

Loose Id® Titles by Sam B. Morgan

Available in digital format at http://www.loose-id.com
or your favorite online retailer

A Rookie Move
Slow Burn

In addition to digital format, the following titles
are also available in print at your favorite bookseller:

Slow Burn